Publisher's Note

Frost Hollow books are aimed at boys between the ages of 11 and 15, though as it turns out, girls seem to enjoy them equally. The series is designed to get boys reading, simply by providing stories they can identify with. To that end the stories include sports, adventure, mystery, suspense, and even romance. The themes are drawn from the things boys experience, though events may, from time to time, explode into either myth or fantasy. Each book is a different story with different characters, and no sequels are planned.

These are not "kids" books where everything is age appropriate, because there is no such thing as an age appropriate kid. They are not written down, but use complex sentence structure and vocabulary which both fit the story and provide some challenge. Nor is there a shortage of the sort of ideas which raise the questions people need to ask. In short, all the elements that any writer of novels uses are used here.

The result is exciting books in which boys are competent, fair-minded, ethical, honest, and even heroic. They also screw up.

Finally, it is important to note that the trend in novels for young adult readers has been to produce books which are designed to be discarded. They are printed on the poorest quality paper which yellows and disintegrates over time.

Frost Hollow books cost a little more, but they are printed on high quality, acid-free paper, meaning they will survive rough handling, backpacks, and time.

After all the book you read and like today is not only a book you may well want to read another day, but a book you might like to save and pass on to your own children. Such things become the threads which bind one generation to another.

D1367120

First Edition

Book Illustration and design by Robert J. Benson
Woodland Creative Group
Vermont

Text set in Times New Roman

Copyright 1998 by Robert Holland
Printed in Quebec, Canada

ISBN 0-9658523-3-4

THE PURPLE CAR

A novel of Mystery and Adventure by
Robert Holland

Keep Reading

FROST HOLLOW
PUBLISHERS, LLC
Woodstock, Connecticut

More
"Books boys want to read"

by Robert Holland

The Voice of the Tree
Summer on Kidd's Creek

Chapter One

For Whom the Bells Toil

He couldn't help it. All morning, he'd been working with his brother and sister and their mother unpacking books and stacking them on the shelves of the library, and he must have carried a hundred empty cartons out to the barn, where he smashed them flat for the recycling center before going back for another load.

And every time he looked down at the pond, winking in the sun like a million diamond eyes, and the field rising up toward the woods far beyond, he felt an urge to go. But each time he trudged back for another load. And then...he didn't. He just turned from the driveway and started out into the field, his feet brushing through the dry stubble of the hay that had been cut three days ago, two days before they had moved into the house in the country they had all dreamed about for so long.

Peter could not have said just what made him head in that particular direction, other than the fact that he had been bored beyond belief and needed a break, but he had the feeling as he walked out onto the rise in the middle of the field, that it was something more. He stopped when he reached the crest of the broad mound and folded his arms over his chest. The July sun fell hot on his head and shoulders as he looked out at the field rolling away from him like an ocean covered with brown stubble.

He was tall for twelve, so tall that people always assumed he was much older, which was cool, except when they also expected him to behave like he was much older. That was not cool, no matter how much he liked being five-ten. And he liked that a lot, especially since it put him two inches above Maria, who was two years older.

Suddenly he felt cold. He shivered and he could feel the hairs stand up on the back of his neck as he shivered again then glanced around, looking behind him, back toward the house. The air was still and hot, the heat waves dancing and wriggling up from the dry field like mad translucent dancing worms. He couldn't hear a sound. The birds were quiet and no cars passed on the road in front of the house. Dead quiet. Peter wondered if he had ever heard such quiet, but whether he had or not, he found that just now it made him uneasy.

And when a crow suddenly called from the far end of the field, he jumped as surely as if it had burst out of a dark closet and flown directly into his face. He whirled in that direction as it called again, and he spotted it sitting at the top of a tall white pine. It looked big, even for a crow, and he wondered if it was a crow. But what else could it be? Ask Brian the brain. The brain would know. If it had anything to do with nature, Brian knew about it.

He stuffed his hands into the pockets of his shorts, wondering what was making him feel so strange, and maybe even a little scared. It was weird. How could you be scared of anything here? And how come he had the feeling that he didn't want to take another step toward the end of the field? What was out there?

This was really stupid! He stepped boldly forward, taking one step and then another, and then he stumbled, his right foot gouging a slash in the ground. Peter stopped, and stepped back to see what he had stumbled on, feeling now as if his feet were glued to the ground. He glanced at his battered Nikes and as he started to look up, something shiny, lying where his foot had dug a slot through the grass, caught his eye, and he squatted, brushing the dirt aside. Slowly his fingers closed on a dull brass cartridge case. He turned it over in his hands looking, at the bottom of the shell. It was hard to read, but he could make out the name Winchester and the numbers forty-five and seventy.

Cool. Really cool. How long had it been here? Who had stood right here and fired a rifle? And what had he been shooting at? A deer? Probably. Dad had said there were lots of deer around.

He swept his hand over the stubble again and found a second case and then a third. Guy must've been a bad shot to have used three shots on a deer. Or maybe it was something else? A gunfight? Wow! He stood up quickly. A gunfight right here in their field! And then he grinned to himself. Imagination. It was just his imagination again, running off crazy the way it always did when something unexplainable came up.

He turned each of the tarnished brass cases, over and over, examining each one closely, but he could not find the shiny spot that had caught his attention. Then he shrugged, dropped the empty cases into his pocket and walked back toward the house, determined to get his mother to take a break from the books so they could all go swimming in the pond. It would be tough though, because once she got into a project, she didn't like to quit until she had finished.

As he walked back toward the house he thought about how neat it would be to have a dog bouncing along beside him. He hoped Mom and Dad hadn't forgotten their promise. Once they moved, they could get a dog. That was the deal. What he had in mind was a big black Labrador retriever and he was sure he could talk Brian into going along with that, but he wasn't so sure about Maria. Somehow he knew she'd have a different idea. She usually did.

He trudged through the large dining room and into the hall that branched to the living room and the library in the front of the house.

"Mom," he said, "I'm really, really hot. Couldn't we go swimming?"

Sarah Bell looked up. "I know its hot, Peter, but I have to finish getting these books unpacked."

Peter looked at the stack of cartons and compared them to the shelves left to fill. "That's gonna take all day," he said.

Sarah finished shelving another row of books. The heat and humidity had made her irritable and Peter was right. They should go swimming. Here they were with their own pond, nobody to bother them, it was almost dead in the middle of summer, and she had them corralled in a stuffy room full of books. This was something they could do after dark. She stood up. "Okay," she said, "you guys get your bathing suits on and

I'll go get the towels...and don't leave your clothes in a pile on the floor. Hang them up!"

They ran for the stairs, screaming and shouting as if they'd been released from prison, and in what seemed like seconds, came tumbling back down and dashed outside, the old screen door slamming shut behind them as they ran down the grassy shallow slope from the house to the narrow sandy beach at the edge of the pond.

The pond covered nearly an acre, and the real estate agent had told them it was over twelve feet deep in the middle. The banks dropped off quickly, and though the water was clear, the bottom was dark, leaving you with the feeling that you couldn't see very far down, even though you could see to the bottom wherever it was light enough to reflect the sunlight.

They stood in line, arranged by height, first Peter, then Maria, who was still not happy about no longer being the tallest, especially since she didn't know anyone who was four-teen and was shorter than their twelve-year-old brother, and finally Brian, who had also begun to stretch out. Pretty soon she'd be the last in line. At least she was taller than Mom.

"Are you sure it's okay?" Maria asked.

"Sure it is," Brian said in his deep matter-of-fact voice. "This is fresh water and it doesn't have anywhere near the kind of stuff that you get in salt water."

"What about snakes?" Maria asked.

"Snakes are scared of people," Brian said.

Maria wanted to trust him, and she was sure he was tell-ing her the truth about the snakes, but still, he was her younger brother. "I'm not going in if there are snakes," she said.

"Jeez, Maria," Peter said. "If Brian says we don't have to worry, then there's nothing to worry about." He stepped into the water. "Look, I'll show you." He waded out, dove in, and swam out into the pond. The water was warm on the surface but just a short way down it was cool to the point of being cold. That was because of the springs in the bottom that kept the pond full. "Look," he called as he turned toward the shore. "No snakes!"

"No snakes," Brian said as he followed Peter into the water, barging in, then diving through the surface and swimming with long powerful strokes out to join his brother. He couldn't run as fast as Maria, and he was no match for Peter at either basketball or baseball, but he could swim like a fish.

Maria waded in. The bottom was sandy and she could see it clearly. That helped. At least she could see them coming. Or did snakes swim on the surface? Why did there have to be snakes anyway? What a dumb idea they were.

Peter and Brian swam back to the shore, standing waist-deep on the sandy bottom. "Com'on, Maria," Peter said. "It's okay, really."

She couldn't see any snakes, and now that she thought about it, she had only seen one snake in her whole life. But if ever she'd seen a place where there ought to be snakes, this was it. She stopped wading when the water reached her waist, looked around, and finally dove in. The temperature was perfect, warm on the surface and cool below.

"This is great, Mom!" Peter shouted as Sarah walked down to the edge of the pond. "Much better than a stupid old pool. This water doesn't hurt your eyes."

Oh my God!" Maria shrieked. "What's that?" She pointed to a small head sticking through the blue surface of the water.

"Painted turtle," Brian said.

"Do they bite?"

He looked at his older sister as if she'd truly lost it. "It's a little painted turtle," he said. "They don't bite." But he couldn't stop there. She was just too vulnerable. "But you gotta watch out for snappers. Sometimes they can get up to forty pounds."

"Are there snappers in here?" Peter asked as he edged closer to shore. Painted turtles he was okay on, but snappers, now snappers were something to worry about.

"Every pond has snappers, but unless you step on their heads, they won't bother you," Brian said. "And they stay in thick mud in the deep parts of the pond."

"What other uglies am I going to find in this pond?" Maria asked.

"Frogs and fish," Brian said. A sly smile flashed across his face. Some things were too good to pass up, and besides, he owed her for all the things she'd done to him — like the time on Halloween when she kept telling him about ghosts and things she wasn't afraid of. "Be careful of the eastern toe biters," he said. "They can give you a nasty pinch. And you wanna watch out for those orange spotted newts too. They've got poison on their skins."

Maria rushed out of the water, throwing a bow wave the equal of a submarine coming ashore. "I'm never going in there again. I don't care if it gets so hot I melt, I'm not going in there again. I wish we had a swimming pool. I never liked swimming in ponds. I like swimming pools!"

"Brian, stop that," Sarah said. "That was mean, making up something like that."

"I didn't make it up," he said. "They're big bugs, about three inches long and they have a pincher in the front, and they bite toes, and they live in the mud." He smoothed the water out of his hair. "Of course you don't have to believe me...."

Sarah looked doubtful. In the first place she had never heard of anything as improbable as an eastern toe biter, and, secondly, she smelled a rat. "And we have them in our pond?"

"Maybe."

"Just...maybe?" His mother raised her eyebrows as she looked around at him, her hands anchored on her narrow hips, sending a clear signal that her tolerance for sister baiting was at an all-time low. When he ignored her signals, she tried voice tone. "Brian?"

"Well, they aren't very common," he said.

"Maria, I think your little brother is settling a score," Sarah said.

"I'll get you for that, dweeb," Maria said as she waded back into the water. "And don't even think about splashing me! I'll drown you like a rat!"

"Maria!" Sarah said. "That's a terrible thing to say."

"Mom," Peter said, "we need a raft to swim out to."

"Talk to your father," she said.

"SNAKE! SNAKE!" Brian shouted at the top of his lungs, and as Peter and Maria scrambled madly up onto the shore, he shouted, "NOOOOOOOOT!"

Chapter Two

"Quothe the Raven..."

Later that afternoon, after Sarah had turned them loose again, Peter led Maria and Brian out into the field. At first they kept to the middle, well out from the thick woods that marked the edges, but as they grew more courageous, they came closer and closer until they could see far into the woods.

They had grown up where houses were set closely together, where the only patch of woods was a park with trails which were wide and easy to follow. Even the brush had been cleared from the small, open patch of woods. You could see the houses on the other side, but here there were no houses, and the woods were thick and dark and dangerous in the way they offered so many places for strange things to hide.

"We sure have a lot of trees," Maria said.

"It's as thick as the woods at Gramma and Grandpa's." Peter looked off between the trees, aware of the shell cases in his pocket, and wondering whether he ought to say anything.

"Typical stand of northern hardwoods," Brian said. "Beech, birch, oak, and maple. White pine where the soil is sandy and hemlock in the hollows where it's wet."

Maria laughed. "How do you know about all this stuff, Bri? Do you get it all out of books, or do you get it from Dad?" She smiled down at him.

"Both," Brian said.

"Hey!" Peter pointed to a corner of the field. "What's that shining in the sun?"

"It looks like glass," Maria said. "Let's go see."

They ran across the field, their feet brushing through the stubble of the hay, driving the dust upward into the hot still air. Suddenly they heard a raspy metallic clatter that sounded as if someone were sawing slowly through metal.

They stopped and turned quickly, and as the sound came again, they looked up toward the top of the old pine at the opposite corner of the field. Even so far away the bird stood out plainly.

"It's a crow," Peter said, turning quickly to his younger brother. "Isn't that right, Brian?"

"It's a raven!" Brian said. "There's not supposed to be ravens here. Too far south."

"How do you know it's not a crow?" Peter asked.

"It's too big and it's feathers stick up on the back of its head, and because crows just don't sound like that." He brushed his blond hair off to one side, only to have it flop back as if it had a life of its own. "One of my videos has ravens on it. That's a raven."

"Cool," Maria said. "Just like the raven in Poe... 'quoth the raven...nevermore...'." She really liked the idea of having a raven around, though she couldn't say why. She just thought it was cool. No. She did know why. Ravens turned up in scary stories almost as often as bats, and ever since she'd outgrown Baby Sitter Club books, she'd been reading scary stories.

Peter shook his head. You could never tell with girls what they'd find to get worked up over.

"It's neat to have a raven," Brian said. "But it's weird to see one so far from where it should be. I'll have to tell Dad about it. When he grew up in New Hampshire they had ravens all around the farm. That's where I first saw them, when he and Grandpa took me for walks."

"Don't do it," Peter said. "If you tell him, then we'll have to sit and listen to more of his stories about growing up in New Hampshire."

"I like those stories," Brian said.

"Booooo," Maria shook her head.

Peter turned away from the raven. "Com'on, let's go find out what's making that reflection."

They were still a hundred feet away when Peter shouted. "Hey! It's an old car." They ran the rest of the way, slowing at the edge of the woods where the brush grew so thick it seemed as if it had been planted there just to keep them out. But their curiosity quickly overrode their fear, and they pushed through, and walked into the open ground beneath the big white oaks where the brush had been shaded out.

It was indeed a car, and they walked around and around it, looking in through the dusty windows, absorbed in discovering each detail, but still keeping a safe distance.

"You know what this'll make? This'll make a dynamite fort!" Peter said. "All we have to do is clean it up a little!"

"Dynamite?" Maria said, her tone of voice making it perfectly clear that Peter had fallen out of the "cool" range. "Nobody uses a word like that. It's pure sixties. God you're beginning to sound like Dad. He's the only person I've ever heard say that!"

He wanted to fight it, but when it came to a choice between doing what Dad did and being cool, there was simply no choice. "Awesome. It'll make a totally awesome fort."

"How did it get here?" Maria said. "And who does it belong to? Why would anyone just leave a car sitting in the middle of the woods? What sense does that make?"

"I don't know," Peter said, "but it's on our land so it must be ours."

Brian looked up and around at his brother and sister. "There's all kinds of cars and trucks in the woods at Gramma and Grandpa's. If you guys did something besides turn into couch potatoes when we go up there, you'd know that. Dad showed me a whole gravel pit of 'em. He used to take parts from 'em to fix other cars when he was in high school."

"Okay, okay," Peter said, impatient now to start a project. He grabbed the handle on the passenger's side door and pulled it downward. The latch clicked but the door refused to open. He braced his foot against the side of the car and pulled as hard as he could, and with a great screech the door came open. "We just need to oil the hinges and then it'll work fine," he said. "I wonder how long it's been sitting here."

Maria, standing near the front of the car, looked down at the door. "What made these holes?" she asked as she squatted down to get a better look, her fingers trailing across the perfectly round holes through the metal.

"Bullets," Brian said.

"Wow," Maria said. "I never saw a bullet hole before.

Look, they went right through the door and into the other door. And they went through the window too." She pointed to the three neat holes through the glass, each with a spider web of cracks radiating outward. There was something fascinating about the way the bullet had chopped such a neat round hole through the glass without shattering the rest of the window.

Peter slid his hand into his pocket, his fingers closing around the cartridge cases. Did the car have something to do with them?

"Who would shoot at an old car?" Maria asked.

"Hunters use 'em for target practice," Brian said.

Peter almost sighed aloud. Of course that was the answer. Some hunter testing out his rifle. It was the only thing that made sense, and he even had the empty shells to prove it. Some hunter had stood out in the field and fired at the car to make sure his gun was sighted in. He climbed into the driver's seat, but he was too excited to sit still, and he jumped out, walked around the front of the car, and opened the passenger door. He tried to wind down the window, but it was rusted solidly in place. "We can oil up the windows and doors and clean off all the dust and it'll make a perfect fort!" He jumped into the car, slid across the seat, wrapped his hands around the steering wheel, and tired to turn it, but the flattened tires held firm, and he could not budge the wheel.

Brian looked down at the bullet holes in the door, noticing how they made a perfect line right up into the window. "These bullet holes are funny," he said.

"Why?" Peter asked.

"The holes I saw in the old cars up in New Hampshire didn't go in a line like this. They were all over the place. But these holes go in a line right up from the bottom of the door and into the window."

"What difference does that make?" Maria asked. She liked the idea of turning the old car into a fort. It'd be cool to have a place out in the woods to go to when she wanted to get away from everyone else, though she wondered whether she'd have courage enough to come all the way out here by herself.

"I don't know," Brian said. "It's just different, that's all." He traced the line with his index finger. "It reminds me of something I saw somewhere, but I can't remember where."

"Okay," Peter said. "Let's make a list of what we need." He pulled a small note pad from his shirt pocket, and slipped a short pencil out of the spiral binding. "First we'll need a screwdriver and oil and stuff to clean up the inside."

"Paper towels," Maria said. "We'll need a whole lot of paper towels and Windex and Fantastic."

"We ought to cut a path from the field," Peter said.

As his brother and sister talked, Brian squatted down, puzzling over the bullet holes. They were too perfectly in line. But there was a reason for that, and it bugged him that he couldn't remember. It would come to him, though, because such things always did.

Brian stood up, then climbed into the car, looking at where the bullets had come through the inside of the door. Only one of them had gone through the other side of the car, and he began looking around inside the car, sliding his hand around on the floor beneath the seat, and then suddenly his fingers closed around a hard piece of metal. He drew it out. "Hey, look what I found!" He held it up as he slid out of the car. "It's a bullet...one of the bullets that made the holes through the door. See the way it's all mashed up on the end where it went through the steel?"

"Cool," Peter said. "Can I see it?"

"I found it," Brian said.

"I just want to look at it, Bri," Peter said.

"Just give it back," Brian said as he handed the chunk of lead to his brother, and then watched closely as Peter turned it over and over in his hand.

Peter wondered what sort of gun it had come from. He didn't know that much about bullets, but this one seemed pretty fat, fat enough even to have come from the cartridge cases he'd found.

"Wow, this is really cool," Peter said as he held it up, trapped between his thumb and index finger. "It's amazingly heavy."

"That's cause it's made of lead," Brian said.

"Jeez, Bri, don't you think I know anything?"

Suddenly from the top of a tree directly overhead the raven's call knifed though the still summer air, and they whipped their heads around and up, looking at the bird sitting, fat and black, thirty feet above them in a dead oak, head cocked to one side, watching them. They could see the light glinting from his black eyes and his heavy black bill.

"It's just the raven," Brian said. "Probably has a nest around here somewhere."

"That is one strange looking bird," Peter said, "and in a weird way, he almost sounds like he's talking."

Maria laughed. "I thought only parrots could talk."

"You guys really don't know anything," Brian said. "Of course ravens can talk. So can crows and Cockatiels and Mynahs, even parakeets!"

"Maybe I like the little birds better," Maria said, "They can't talk and they don't look like they're on their way to a funeral."

Chapter Three

Things Get Bloody Strange

Perhaps it was the unique quality of their new fort, or perhaps some greater force which drew them back at least once a day, but no such question arose. They saw it simply as a great adventure; an adventure of the sort best suited to summer vacations. They cleared away the broken glass and the dust which had seeped in over the years. They wiped the grime from the windows, and they drove out the mice just with their presence.

For a week they spent the better part of each day at the fort, always finding something else to clean or repair. Peter brought out an oil can and oiled the doors till they opened and closed without a sound. Maria washed the windows till they were as clean as they had been when the car was new. Brian wiped and wiped at the old paint, and though he managed to remove the dirt and dust, no matter how hard he rubbed, the surface of the car looked the same, an odd dark purple, something close to the color of a withered grape.

Maria thought it was beautiful, but her brothers thought it was the ugliest color they had ever seen. In the end, of course, the color really didn't matter all that much, because the color had little to do with what was, without question, the most exciting fort ever. They had never heard of a fort to equal it. Even so, after a week the novelty began to wear off, and by the following week they visited the car less and less.

Part of that had to do with the growing heat of July which kept them close to the pond or inside where they read, played video games, or watched the movies their mother rented. It was just too hot to walk all that way across the field in the blazing sun, only to sit around in the car trying to think of a game. And that, of course, was the biggest single trouble with that fort or any fort. Once the work is done, once it's been used as a base for all the games you can think of, the fort begins to fade in importance.

Yet each of them in their own way felt drawn back to the odd purple car, though they did not to go, nor did they talk about it, and that too was unusual. The car was just *there*, out at the end of the field, guarded by the raven, or so they believed, and in a way it was like the early twinges of a toothache. The pain doesn't go away and becomes a reminder that sooner or later you're going to have to take care of it.

Their father, Tom, took the last week of July off to work on the house, trying to get enough done so they could spend the last week of August up in New Hampshire.

For a couple of days the boys followed Tom around, trying to help, but mostly getting in his way. Maria helped Sarah inside, and then she helped weed the flower gardens. By the third day they were bored...flat out, completely and totally bored, flopping from chair to chair, activity to activity as if they were sleep-walking. The one thing they didn't do was complain. Complaining only resulted in work.

Each day they got up later and later, and that left them having to scrounge some breakfast, which they ate by themselves at the kitchen table.

"Let's go out to the fort," Maria said as she dipped the spoon into her cereal. "We haven't been there in at least a week. Maybe we can take our lunch too."

"Cool," Peter said.

"Double cool," Brian said as he took a bite of English muffin. "The more we hang around, the more work we get."

"I wonder if the raven's still there," Maria said. She finished her cereal and picked up her English muffin, looking suspiciously at the red jelly as if perhaps she'd been served some deadly concoction. "What kind of jelly is this?"

"Blood!" Peter said as he tried to imitate what the vampires sounded like in the movies. "I gathered it especially for our breakfast so ve vill not lose the energy...."

"Cool! Blood jelly! Yeah, all right!" Brian took particular delight in using those words which sent Maria into spasms of disgust.

"Ugh," Maria said. "I think I'm gonna puke."

"Cool," Brian said. Bodily fluids of any description also provided endless attraction. It was just like the insides of things. Once you peeled the skin away from a worm or a frog there were amazing things to see.

"What's cool?" Tom asked as he came into the kitchen carrying a bucket of plumbing tools and supplies.

"Blood jelly," Peter said, using his finest vampire imitation. "I vas up the whole night, gathering the blood of virgins, especially to make the blood jelly for the breakfast."

Tom laughed. "Sounds delicious." He held up his plastic pail. "Anybody interested in plumbing?" No answer. "Somehow I didn't think I'd get any takers on that one. Too many spiders." He laughed and walked on into the dining room, heading for the cellar stairs.

"Haven't you guys finished eating yet?" Sarah asked as she carried clean dish towels and napkins into the kitchen.

"We're going out to our fort," Peter said.

"Can we take a lunch?" Maria asked.

"Why don't you come back for lunch, and then we can all go swimming. I'm sure your father will be looking forward to a swim after he gets through in the cellar."

"Okay," Maria said as she pushed back her chair. "We'll be back in time for lunch." She picked up her dishes and carried them to the sink, and then turned and looked at her brothers. "Com'on guys, bring the dishes over so I can put them into the dishwasher." She could hear them grumbling behind her as they picked up their bowls and glasses and carried them to the sink. It was worth having to load the stuff into the dishwasher, just to hear them grumble.

They had reached the halfway point in the field when the raven began talking. He seemed louder than before, and much busier, calling and gurgling at them in a steady stream of nasal, high-pitched sounds. In the still, hot air he seemed especially loud, his calls ringing in their ears and echoing off the solid wall of the trees on the far side of the field. When he stopped, the silence seemed to close in about them. No other birds sang, and even the insects seemed to have sought the shelter of the shade. Then he started again, louder, more harsh and strident and commanding.

"Listen to that," Brian said. "There must be an owl or a hawk nearby."

"An owl?" Maria said.

"Ravens hate owls. Owls raid their nests," Brian said.

"Do you really think we have owls too?" Peter asked.

"Jeez, don't you guys listen to anything. You can hear them every night. There's barred owls and great horned owls and even screech owls."

"I'm not into owls," Maria said.

"Then why do you stay up so late?" Peter said. "Mom says you're a regular night owl."

"Oh, piss off, Peter."

He laughed, delighted to have had his jibe find a target, even if he had not really meant it as an attack.

As they approached the car, they could see that something had changed, but not until they reached it did they see how much had changed. The faded purple color was now a deep, glossy black covered with a fine dust. The tires were fully inflated, and the wide white sidewalls were almost painfully bright. And they could see the track where the car had been dragged in from the field and abandoned.

"It looks brand new," Brian said.

"But how could that happen?" Maria stepped back as if she were afraid to get too close.

"Oh man, this has suddenly gone and gotten really spooky," Peter said. "Wow, I mean like really spooky... and really weird." He stayed close to Maria. "Stuff like this happens in movies and books, but not in real life. Nothing like this ever happens in real life, and if it did, I'd be scared, and maybe that's why I'm scared."

"Too spooky," Maria said. "Way too spooky." She stepped farther away from the car.

"Must be a ghost." Brian shugged. "No other way to explain it."

"A ghost couldn't do something like that," Peter said. "And anyway, Brian, there's no such thing as ghosts."

The driver's side door was open, and he could see the glass on the seats, and the old stain they had noticed before on the back of the seat was now red, and it looked wet.

"Hey," Peter called, "look at this!"

"I'm not coming any closer," Maria said, "and I'm not looking at anything." She covered her eyes, started to turn her back to the car, and then thought better of it. All she wanted to do was run, but something held her there as if her shoes had been screwed to the ground.

"But you gotta see this!"

Brian walked around the car, his curiosity running wild as he stood next to, but slightly behind, his older brother. There was no doubt in his mind that a ghost had been at work, because it was just the sort of stuff you'd expect a ghost to do, no matter what Peter said.

"Com'on, Maria, just take a quick look."

Without coming an inch closer to the car, Maria circled through the brush, stepping over and around the rotting trunks of trees which had fallen long, long ago, until she stood next to Peter and Brian. Peter pointed to the red smear on the seat. "What do you think that is?"

"I don't have any idea," Maria said. "No. That's not true. I do have an idea, but I don't want to look at it, and more than that, a lot more than that, I don't want to think about it."

"Blood." Brian leaned closer. "Looks pretty fresh too. Maybe several hours old. You can tell because it hasn't changed color yet, and it's still shiny."

"That's it! I'm outta here." Maria turned and barged on through the thick brush and out into the field. "Are you coming?"

Brian walked back around to the passenger side of the car and looked at the line of bullet holes that swept up the door and into the window. "Hey, Peter, remember that movie we saw about those gangsters and what the car looked like after the hit man shot it with a machine gun? Well that's what these bullet holes look like. I'll bet some big-time gangster was shot in this car."

"And now his ghost has come back to haunt it?"

"Yeah."

"Cool."

Suddenly, directly over head the raven cut loose and they both jumped.

"That bird is weird," Peter said. "Sometimes he sounds almost human."

"Of course it might not be human blood," Brian said. "Remember the coon that got hit in the road? Suppose there was another one and he came out here and hid in the car."

"I don't think so, Bri," Peter said. "For one thing the blood is too high up on the seat, and there's too much of it. But even if you were right about the raccoon, how would you explain what happened to the paint and the tires and all the rest."

Brian nodded. "I'm getting a little scared now," he said as he began moving backward away from the car. "I'm going with Maria."

Without another word they turned and started to run, dashing from the fringe of woods and into the field, and Maria needed no invitation, but took off for the house, her long, skinny legs keeping her well out ahead of her brothers.

Within a couple of strides, Peter had left Brian behind, struggling along on his shorter thicker legs and hollering, "Wait up! Wait up you dickheads!"

But neither of them stopped until they were well out of sight of the car and only then did they turn to watch Brian chugging along. His body looked like he was running fast as any rabbit, but only very slowly did he draw closer. And just as he reached them, they turned to take off again.

"Hey, wait! Whatcha running for? You can't even see it from here!"

Maria stopped and reached out to him. "Hurry, Brian!"

They raced the rest of the way to the yard which surrounded the house, running as if something were chasing them, snapping at their heels. They ran, after that, as fast as Brian could run, needing to outrun their imaginations, dashing across the freshly mowed lawn around to the south side of the house to come tumbling through the open cellar door, and down to where Tom was running a new water line to the kitchen for the ice maker in the refrigerator.

Out of breath, gobbling and gabbing like a flock of startled turkeys, all three talking at the same time, they tried to explain what they had seen. But there was no way Tom could make sense of their energized magpie chatter.

"Whoa," Tom said, "calm down. I can't understand anything you're saying."

They stopped, but only for a second, and then almost at the same instant started again, louder this time, each one trying to shout the other down. And with all three voices at different pitches not a single word came out clearly enough for their father to understand.

"Whoa," Tom said again. "You've got to do this one at a time." They stopped. "Now, who's going to go first?" A chorus of me's nearly blew the screens off the basement windows. All three kids jumped up and down clamoring to be first, their hands shooting up for recognition as if they were still in school.

Tom laughed and Maria brought him up sharply. "Dad, this is serious!" she shouted. "This is nothing to laugh at! You have to listen!"

He sobered instantly. Maria took most things seriously, but seldom did she sound frightened, and that was what he now heard in her voice.

"Okay, Maria," he said, his voice low and quiet, "tell me what happened."

She managed to get through the story with only two interruptions from Peter, who added the details he felt were particularly important.

At the end, Brian chimed in with his two cents worth, though it was more like a dollar. "Yup," he said, "it was blood all right, and plenty of it. Looked like the work of a ghost to me, but you can never be sure about these things. Could've been a troll of some kind."

Tom picked up his coffee cup, drained it, looked at the plumbing job that now would most certainly be delayed, and looked down at his kids. "Maybe the best thing," he said, "is to go have a look." He took off his tool belt, hung it from a nail driven into one of the floor joists, and started for the door. When no one followed he turned and looked around at them. "Are you coming?"

"I don't know," Maria said.

Peter stuck his hands into the pockets of his jeans. "It was pretty scary. Maybe if you just went out and had a look by yourself, Dad."

"Nothing but an old ghost," Brian said.

"You didn't sound so brave when you got left behind in the field," Peter said

. "I just didn't want to be last," Brian said.

Tom grinned and started up out of the hatchway. "Com'on," he said, "we'll all go have a look. I think I need to see what's there before your imaginations run completely out of control."

Together, very close together, they marched across the field, walking a diagonal line to where the pines formed a peninsula that reached out from the woods and screened a large rectangular piece of the field from the house. The car sat at the far corner of the rectangle.

The hay had started to turn green now, and it was already hard to remember how it had looked that first day, so brown and dry and dead, the grass clipped crew cut short.

Once past the pines, Maria pointed. "There," she said. "You can see the sunlight on the windows." Even from seventy yards away, Maria knew that something was different, but not until they pushed aside the brush and walked up to the car did she know how different. The car was purple again, and it looked just as it had before they had converted it into a fort. The paint was dull and old, and the blood on the back of the seat had faded back to an unrecognizable brown stain. But how could that be? Had they imagined it all? No. Not a chance. After all, each of them had seen the same thing, and that simply wasn't the way imagination worked.

"Looks like an abandoned 1940 Ford coupe," Tom said, "and in surprisingly good shape. Now where's all this blood?"

"It was on the driver's seat," Maria said. "On the back of the seat, but I think it's gone now."

Tom opened the door and looked at the seat and the large dark stain in the very middle of the back rest. It was old and the velour seat material was badly faded, but the stain showed clearly. He ran his hand over it, and then, near one edge, hidden by a fold in the cloth he found a hole. He walked back around to the passenger side, looking at the line of bullet holes that tracked from a point halfway up the door and into the window. Slowly now, he circled the car, exploring it closely. He found a bullet embedded in the door post on the driver's side and two more holes in the door near the very bottom. He climbed into the car and sat behind the wheel. "I have to admit this is pretty strange," he said. "The odometer is still under a hundred miles, and I'd say from looking at the car, that it was brand new when it ended up here."

"Probably a bank robber who got in a shootout with the cops," Brian said.

Tom grinned. "Well you could be right about that, Brian, but there's probably another, much less exciting explanation." He climbed out of the car and walked around to the back, looking down at the old license plate. "This is pretty interesting," he said as he crouched, and taking a rag from his back pocket, wiped away fifty-eight years of dirt and grime. "Connecticut, 1940."

"That means the car really was new when it was left here, doesn't it?" Maria asked.

"I sure would think so," he said.

"Did you see the bullet holes?" Peter asked. He walked around to the side of the car and squatted down to get a better look. "Brian said hunters wouldn't make a line of holes like that."

Tom looked down at the holes. "I think he's right about that. Looks like they were made with a machine gun." He rubbed his chin. "You know, I'd like to find out more about this car, and I know just who to ask. Walter Barbour."

"The old man down the road?" Maria asked.

"He's pretty mean looking," Peter said. "And he's got a mean old dog too."

"But I'll bet he can tell us about this car. Let's go get some lunch, and I'll give him a call. Maybe if he's not doing anything this afternoon we can pay him a visit." He looked at his watch. "Best we get a move on. Your mother will have lunch waiting."

They started across the field, walking abreast.

"I'll bet if we looked hard enough we could find the money," Brian said. "It's gotta be there. I figure he must have been a bank robber, and he stuck up a bank, most likely in Putnam, and he was making his getaway when he got spotted by the cops, who jumped into their cars and took off after him. He probably didn't know the area very well and he took a wrong turn, and when he got to the end of the field they had him trapped, and all he could do was shoot it out with them."

"What makes you think that's what happened?" Tom asked.

"It's perfectly logical, Dad," Brian said. "Anyone can see that."

Tom grinned. "Maybe, but then not everyone's got your imagination, you know." He reached out and ruffled Brian's blond hair. "I thought you guys had fixed that place up. Mom says you used up a bottle of window cleaner, a jug of Fantastic and three rolls of paper towels."

"We did," Maria said. "That's why it's all so spooky."

Chapter Four

Walter Barbour's Odd Tale

Because the kids were afraid of the big old ugly dog, they drove to Mr. Barbour's house, and when he came out onto his porch to meet them, the big old dog turned out to be not the least bit ugly, but instead nearly wore himself out wiggling with excitement.

"Lo there," Walter Barbour said, "don't mind old Wally, can't stand anyone on a bicycle, but once they come to ground he recognizes them as people." He was a small man, roundly built, with a large stomach. His fine hair was nearly pure white, and his blue eyes twinkled brightly in the sun.

"Tom Bell," their father said as he reached out and shook hands. "Appreciate your taking the time to get us straightened out on this." He grinned. "You know how kids are. Full of imagination."

"Good chance to meet my new neighbors."

"This is Maria and Peter and Brian."

"Hello there again," Mr. Barbour said, shaking hands with each of them. "You're just about the ages of my grand-children, I'd guess." He asked each of them what grade they were in. When he spoke, he looked directly at them, and his voice was warm and friendly, and he sounded much as you would expect a grandfather to sound. "Now," he said, "let's go into the house, because unless my nose has deceived me, Martha has made some of her very best sugar cookies and a pitcher of fresh lemonade." He turned to Tom. "Might's well call me Walt, everyone does."

They sat around the big oak table in the kitchen. The room smelled of freshly baked cookies, and from the windows you could see to the large pond below where a small herd of Holsteins grazed across a bright green pasture.

"I didn't know you were still farming," Tom said.

"Not. Morton Barker ran out of pasture for his heifers, so I offered him my pastures. Nice to see the animals graz-ing," he said. "Specially when I don't have to milk 'em. Forty years was enough."

"Well, hello there," Martha Barbour said as she walked quickly into the kitchen. She was as thin as Walt was round, but her smile was every bit as warm.

"Now," she said, after the introductions were complete, "would anyone here like some cookies and lemonade? Or are you still too full from dinner?"

The "yes pleases" were unanimous, and as she carried the lemonade and the cookies to the table, Walt leaned back into his chair and began the story.

"To be sure, this is an odd tale," he said. "Most likely the strangest thing that ever happened in Woodstock. Nineteen forty it was..." he looked over at the calender. "Well now there's a coincidence. It was on this very day in July just fifty-eight years ago." He shook his head. "Quite a coincidence," he said again, but he sounded just the least bit uncomfortable, as people sometimes do when events coincide and appear to give them meaning they don't have. "Well, let's see now, where was I. Oh, yes. Been a terrible hot summer, dry, dry as a bone. Hadn't had a bit of rain since the middle of June, and we were right on the edge of losing the corn. But it was a fine year for hay and Hec — Hector Chandler, who lived in your place then — Hec was just a day or two from haying the back lot.

"In those days there was another road between here and your drive that Hec used to haul out timber with his horses. Didn't have a tractor." He paused. "Said tractors didn't understand him." He reached for a cookie, letting his joke sink in, and when they all chuckled, he took a bite and went on talking. "The road was gravel then, and most of the year, especially during mud time in the spring, it was rough. Seldom saw much traffic. Once a week maybe a car went past.

"That day the temperature got up to a hundred and two by dinner time, and the air was dead still and so humid that just walking from the house to the barn seemed like a day's toil. Too hot to work, and I'd settled onto the veranda with a book and a pitcher of lemonade." He grinned. "Be dogged if I don't think it was this very pitcher. Is that right, Martha?"

"It was," she said. "The very one."

"Coincidences thick as black flies in April," Walt said. He picked up his glass and sipped the lemonade. "As it turned out, even Hec, who was a demon for work no matter the weather, had taken to his porch too. Finding two Yankee farmers in the middle of a summer day sitting on their porches was unusual enough, but it was the heat, you see. Couldn't work in heat like that, at least not here in New England where we're not used to it." He looked over at Maria and Peter and Brian sitting on the edges of their chairs, and satisfied that he'd got the suspense just right, he went on.

"Well there I was, sitting on the porch reading my book when down the road I heard a car coming fast. It was making a terrible clatter, kicking up stones into the fender wells, the tires banging over the ruts and holes in the road, and I got so curious I set down my book and walked to the rail of the porch to get a better look.

"Closer and closer it come, and I was getting more and more curious all the time, and then suddenly it come a-hammering down the hill and went past, throwing a cloud of dust clear to the top of the trees. One man driving, nobody else in the car. He was wearing a gray fedora, and he sat kind of low in the seat, and the car was a Ford, looked to be brand new. Still don't know how he kept it on the road. Never seen a car go so fast even on a good road.

"Now no sooner does he go charging past then I hear another car coming. And while I was waiting, I heard the Ford make a wrong turn onto Hec's tote road instead of taking the fork to the right, and I says to myself, there'll be some trouble over that all right, because if it was one thing you had to know about Hec, he had no tolerance for trespassers. Wouldn't even say it in the Lord's Prayer. Went to 'debtors' long before the Reverend Potts finally decided to switch, because it sounded like the church was full of serpents. Anyway, I was just getting through that thought, when here come the second car, running every bit as fast and wild as the first one. This was a big black Cadillac, and it had three men in it, all of them dressed like they was going to a funeral, and I thought they looked like they'd been to quite a few."

He paused for another bite of cookie and a sip of lemonade, thoroughly enjoying the rapt attention of his audience. "Well, I guess the fella driving the Caddy must've seen the dust in the air, because danged if he didn't follow that other car right onto Hec's tote road. Now that road runs in and forks, one to the left going up into the woods, and the other going past the back of the barn. The left fork had a gate on it to keep the cows in, so the cars had to take the right fork past the back of the barn." He smoothed back his unruly white hair. "I knew sure as a bred cow freshens, there was trouble coming, and I dashed into the house and grabbed my thirty-thirty. 'By golly,' I called out to Martha, 'there's some trouble starting up to Hec's! You see if you can get the State Troopers on the phone 'cause unless I miss my guess, Hec's got two car loads of desperadoes smack in the middle of his hay lot.' Then I jumped into my truck and took off after 'em.

"I was halfway to the bottom of the hill when the shooting started. Never heard such shooting, whole bunch of shots right close together like beads on a necklace. I stepped on the gas and went wailing into the tote road, and just as I slowed toward the back of the barn I heard Hec's old forty-five-seventy bark once and then twice more. As I pulled into the hayfield I could see Hec standing right out in the open sighting down his rifle, and I stopped and grabbed my rifle and ran toward where the pines stick out into the middle of the field, figuring that I'd come on 'em from the flank in case they'd got hunkered down behind the cars.

"Time I got to the other side of the trees I was soaked right through with sweat as if I'd been running in the rain.

And it was some sight I saw then. Hec was standing off a hundred and fifty yards or so, and there was two men lying dead, one thrown up onto the hood of the car, and another leaning against a back wheel. Third man was huddled behind the Caddy with a little pistol which was just about no use a'tall at that range. On the other hand, Hec couldn't get a clear shot at him, and it'd come down to a perfect standoff.

"But I could see him right clear, and I put my old Savage to my shoulder. 'Drop that pistol,' I cried out, 'drop it or I'll drop you dead as the others!' He let it go, but he was shot in the leg, and he couldn't stand. Besides, Hec was standing right out there in the middle of the field with that forty-five-seventy solid to his shoulder. That rifle sounded more like a cannon than a rifle.

"I called out, 'Hec! I got the drop on him,' I says.

"Hec was still pretty excited, and it was a good bet he'd just gun the man down once he got something to shoot at. So I called out again. 'Hec,' I says, 'don't you shoot him. Troopers are coming and he's dropped his gun. What the devil's going on here?'."

"'Killin's what's going on here, Walter, and I'm the one that's doing it! Got two and I'll get the third one too, soon's I get a clear shot.'

" 'Hec,' I says, 'He's throwed away his pistol.' It was quiet for a time, and then finally Hec spoke. 'I'll not shoot him then, Walter,' he called back. 'Wouldn't shoot an unarmed man, but get him into the open where he can be watched. There's maybe one more there you can't see!'

"The third desperado was sorely wounded." He shook his head once and clicked his tongue. "Forty-five-seventy makes a God-awful big hole. Bone was all busted up inside and blood running every which way. So we let him sit, leaning against the car while we waited for the troopers. Then we picked up all the guns and walked over to have a look into the Ford. We'd been so busy with the third desperado that we'd altogether forgotten about the first one.

"The car was pretty well shot up with a line of machine gun bullets having tracked right up the door and through the passenger side window. We expected to find another body, but all we found was a lot of blood on the back of the driver's seat. We found where the man had crawled off through the high grass, keeping the car between himself and Hec.

"'He's sorely wounded,' I said. 'Most likely lying up in the woods with his pistol at the ready.'

" 'Bleed out soon enough'," Hec said.

"I got my truck, and we hauled the wounded man back to the house. By then Martha had got there, and she and Hec's wife, May, come out to see whether we'd been shot.

"Then while we waited for the police, May and Martha did what they could to make the desperado comfortable till the police could get him to a hospital, but it was plain to see he was dying, though he didn't know it yet. Never saw an uglier human being. Pock marks he had, covered his whole face, and three nasty looking scars, and his nose had been broken so it was bent bad to the left. Short he was, not much larger than a teenaged boy.

"Dying or not, Hec wanted some answers, as well a man might who's just killed two men and most likely, a third. Hard to hear what he answered, and Hec had to get right down close to his mouth, but then Hec's hearing had suffered from too many years of running his little sawmill, while my hearing was quite sharp, and I heard every word.

"Wasn't long before he'd got too weak to talk and not long after that he breathed his last.

"We were sitting in the kitchen drinking lemonade when the Troopers finally got there, two cars of 'em, sirens howling like banshees, lights-a-flashing...quite a sight." He reached for his glass of lemonade.

Brian couldn't hold it in a second longer. "Were they bank robbers?" His eyes were wide as a startled owl. "They must've been bank robbers because bank robbers always carried machine guns back then. In violin cases. They always carried them in violin cases."

Walt grinned. "Now, just hold your horses there, young fella, I'm getting to that part." He sipped his lemonade, took a deep breath, and picked up where he had left off. "The troopers went out with us to look things over, and then one of them came back and used his radio to call for Cranky Joe Fish to come down with his bloodhounds. They picked up on the trail all right, but it led right down to the bog out back of the hayfield. You couldn't go in there. Nothing went out onto that bog. One second you're walking on solid ground, the next you're under the bog and into the water. Get caught under that mat on the top of the bog, you never can get out.

"They circled the bog, time and again, but no trail came out so they figured he'd fallen through and that was that. But the story doesn't end there, exactly. We found out later from the Troopers that the four of them belonged to a gang in Hartford that controlled all the illegal gambling and other illegal activities. But what the Troopers didn't know was what the wounded desperado told Hec. Seems they'd had a falling out, and the fella in the Ford had lit out with a bundle of money, but he didn't hardly get out the door before they took up the chase. Said it could have been as much as a million dollars in cold cash. Course back then a million dollars bought a good deal more than it does today, but it's still nothing to sneeze at." He pulled himself up in his chair. "They'd chased him all the way from Hartford, but they never got close enough to shoot until he come up onto a dead end in Hec's hay lot. That's when they cut loose with the machine gun, and that's when Hec got the drop on 'em. Wasn't anyone who could shoot like Hec. Even with that old cannon of a Winchester he was good out to two hundred yards.

"Turned out they were all wanted by the police and Hec got a check for ten thousand dollars from the FBI. He offered to split it with me, but I told him I hadn't done anything to deserve it. Still, he said it was me got the drop on the third man so that meant I ought to get at least a third of the money, and he took out a great wad of bills, more money that I ever saw in my life, and right then and there counted out thirty-three hundred dollars. Most money I ever got in one chunk in my life." Walt leaned back in his chair. "Now isn't that a scorcher of a story?"

Tom spoke first. "It's got to be the goshdarndest story I ever heard! Now I know why the town clerk looked at me so strangely when I went up to get my dump permit."

Walt smiled. "Bessie is Hec and May's youngest daughter. For a long time some wild stories went around about ghosts in the hay lot, but they were just stories. Hec just laughed at them. 'There was two big battles among Indians fought in that very place,' he said, 'and I'd guess if I haven't seen any Indian ghosts, I'll not likely see ghosts of any other kind'."

"What happened to the money?" Maria asked.

"Never found a dollar of it. And don't think we didn't look. Oh, we looked all right, but most likely he had it with him when he broke through the bog and drowned. Bad place, that is. Place you ought to stay away from. Deep. Fifty maybe a hundred feet in places, and treacherous all around the edges.

The Troopers come in with a boat and tried to drag the open water for the body with a grapple, but they give up after a couple of days. The grapple kept snagging on the bottom and they couldn't get the boat into the mat that floats on the bog." He smiled. "Strange to think there could be a million dollars sitting on the bottom of that bog and nobody can get to it. Makes quite a good mystery. Course, he could have ditched the money somewhere along the way too, just tossed it out the window, though that never seemed likely to me.

"Always puzzled me how a thing like that could happen. All the possible turns in the road he could have taken between here and Hartford, and he winds up in Hec's hay lot. Any place else, probably would've come out a lot different, because most nobody else would've been so quick to his gun as Hec, and not many around shot nearly so well. Stranger still, he gets shot, walks out onto the only quaking bog in this whole part of the state, and flat out disappears."

"How did the car get into the woods?" Peter asked.

"Hec towed it there with his horses. Nobody ever came to claim it. I asked him why he didn't patch up the holes, fix the window, and drive it, and he said it was a jinxed machine. Brand new car. Had less than a hundred miles on it. Only the one side was shot up. Troopers towed the Caddy away, but they left the Ford, and I never did find out why. Just left it."

"Who were they?" Brian asked.

"Never knew the names of the men in the Caddy, but the little fella in the Ford was a terrible cold blooded killer named Little Louie LaMontaigne. He was wanted for murder in ten states. They were all killers, but he was the worst. Kind of strange to think that in the end they couldn't take the measure of a lone farmer with his rifle. Hec was sixty when that happened, and he lived to be ninety-five. Tough as nails, he was.

Lived right there by himself after May died. Then he caught pneumonia one winter and went into the hospital. Never come out." He shook his head, his white hair flopping gently. "Don't make 'em like that anymore. Even then they didn't make many like Hector Chandler."

◆ ◆ ◆

They rode quietly home, all of them thinking over what they had heard. As they turned into the driveway, Tom said, "when you tell Mom the story, you ought to take turns. This time Peter gets to go first, then Brian, then Maria. Okay?"

"I never get to go first," Brian said.

"You can go first in my place," Peter said.

Brian looked up at his older brother in complete disbelief. "You mean that?"

"You tell up to where Mr. Barbour chased after the cars with his thirty-thirty, then I'll tell about the gunfight, and Maria can tell about the bog and the lost money."

Brian thought it over. "No," he said, "I want to tell about the gunfight." He sounded as if he thought he'd been tricked.

"Okay," Peter said, "then I'll go first."

"Okay," Brian said, but you could tell from his voice that he still wasn't sure whether he'd been duped or not. Older brothers and sisters were pretty tricky. You could never be careful enough. One slip and you ended up getting the worst end of every deal.

And of course Tom had to sort it all out again when they came scrambling through the door into the kitchen as wild and electric as kids on a Christmas morning mission to find out what Santa has brought.

Sarah got the story, though it took a good deal longer to

tell than when Mr. Barbour had gotten through it with but a single interruption.

Surprisingly, it lost little in the retelling for Sarah was every bit as mesmerized as they had been. And yet, she seemed to treat it as if it were pure myth. "You don't really think that happened, do you?"

"I don't know what to think," Tom said. "I can't think why Walt would lie."

"Well you know the old timers better than I do," Sarah said. "God knows you grew up with them."

"That I did," Tom said, "and I can tell you this. There wasn't one of them didn't like a good story, and to be sure, they embellished them over the years, but they didn't make their stories up. They were real stories, about things that happened, and they were important because they were meant to be told to kids growing up so they'd know something about what life was like."

"I found something that might help," Peter said. He stood up, took the cartridge cases from his pocket and dropped them onto the table. "I found them in the field right where Mr. Barbour said Hec stood. Forty-five seventy. Three of 'em." He picked one up and showed his father the butt end of the case. "See, it says right there. Winchester 45-70.

"Wow..." Brian said. "Just like Mr. Barbour told us."

"Now don't go jumping to any wild conclusions," Sarah said. But it was already far, far too late for that. There was no question. The story was true. "And don't get any funny ideas. You know what Mr. Barbour said about that bog. If I'd known about that, we'd never have bought this house."

Tom grinned. "Good thing to know about, a bog."

Chapter
Five

New Friends

All that night and into the next morning they could talk of nothing else. They went over it and over it, recounting the story, so absorbed in making sure they had every detail down, that they hardly had time to acknowledge their parents, or even their breakfast.

And always they came back to one part of the story...the body in the bog. They could see the old bones lying there — a perfect skeleton — the skin, and the flesh long ago eaten away by turtles and eels (as Brian pointed out), the bones stained by the water, partly buried by leaves and rotted reeds. It was so wonderfully gruesome that there was no way they could let go of it. Each retelling led to another round of possible explanations, their imaginations exploding outward as they thought up greater and greater horrors, but in the end it always came down to one thing. What had happened to the money? Was it sitting there next to the bones in the bog in some kind of bag, or had he buried it before he went out onto the bog, or had it simply rotted away?

"What we need to know first," Peter said, "is what killed him first. Was it the bullet wound or did he fall through the bog right away and drown?"

"I think he drowned," Maria said. "I think he went out onto the bog and fell through. And he'd been shot, and he got under the stuff on top of the bog, and didn't have the strength to fight his way out."

"But he was called Little Louie," Peter said, "and maybe he was so little that he got a long way out onto the bog, and then he heard people looking for him, and he just lay there hidden in the stuff that grows on the top of the bog, waiting for them all to leave before he made his next move. I'll bet there's a lot of places where the bushes on the bog are thick enough to hide in, especially for a little guy."

"Leatherleaf," Brian said. "Some people call it Labrador tea. There are all kinds of interesting plants that grow in quaking bogs. I'll bet if we looked hard enough we could even find some pitcher plants, even if they're not very common in this part of New England."

Maria turned and looked at him. "God, Bri, it's like living with an automatic CD ROM. Plug him in, boot him up, and watch him spout information."

"Beats being a total airhead."

"Enough!" Sarah said.

"Pitcher plants are totally cool. They collect water in the flower, bugs get in and drown, and then they eat the bugs."

Peter was impatient with the interruption. "Whatever," he said, before remembering how much his mother hated that word. It produced her standard reaction.

"Not, whatever," she said. "Pitcher plants."

"Okay, okay, Mom, jeez, give it a rest, will you?"

"How's that?" Tom said as he walked into the kitchen carrying his coffee and the morning paper.

"I've decided," Sarah said, "that we are going up to Barrett's Pond, to the town beach. It's time you got a chance to meet some of the kids you'll be in school with, and I can't think of a more likely place to find them."

"Good idea," Tom said.

Maria, Peter, and Brian went silent, staring down at the table, knowing they'd blown it.

"I think it's a great idea," Tom said, trying to generate some enthusiasm.

"I don't," Maria said.

"Me neither," Peter said.

"Yeah," Brian said, "probably nothing but weird teenage boys and girls with cooties."

Maria looked up. How could she not have thought of that? She switched sides. "Maybe I was wrong," she said. "Maybe it's a good idea to go meet some other kids. I mean, we do live here now." What she didn't admit, because she was not about to give her brothers any ammunition, was that Brian was right. Boys hung out at beaches, and she was definitely interested in cute boys, especially cute older boys who could drive and were taller than all the dweebs her age, because at five-eight, tall boys were critical.

"Okay," Sarah said, "it's eight-thirty now. I'll clean up here, pack a lunch, and we'll leave in one hour sharp."

"You'll have to stop at the town hall to pick up a beach

sticker for the car," Tom said.

"Right! Beach sticker."

"I can probably catch some different kinds of bugs and frogs," Brian said. He pushed back from the table. "I'll have to pack my stuff."

"You're *not* bringing that stuff," Maria said.

Brian looked around at her. "Why not?"

"Because I'm not going to have everybody there thinking I've got this nerdy little brother who goes around touching slimy gross things."

Peter grinned. "She's afraid the boys will think she's weird because she's got a weird brother."

"I'm not weird," Brian said.

"I didn't mean you're weird," Peter said quickly. "I just meant that Maria's afraid some cute boy will *think* you are and he won't talk to her."

"Peter, you are a jerk!" Maria said as she stood up and rushed out of the kitchen.

"That wasn't very nice, Peter," Sarah said.

"I'll go talk to Maria," Sarah said. "Tom, will you please explain to Peter why what he just said was absolutely cruel and completely uncalled for, and that he can't treat his sister that way."

Tom sat down at the table and scratched his head, as he tried to figure out how to start. What made it hard was that as far as he could see, Peter had told the truth, and that was what had gotten to Maria. Maybe that was the tack to take. "Peter, sometimes," he said, "sometimes it's just better not to tell the truth. I don't mean you should lie, I mean don't say anything. You see sometimes with girls..."

"No lecture, okay, Dad? She just gets her feelings hurt too easy, that's all."

"But part of being a family is trying not to hurt each other's feelings," Tom said.

Brian watched the conversation as if it were a tennis match, turning his head as his father spoke, and again as Peter answered. But it all seemed kind of silly. "Tell Maria not to wear her heart on her sleeve," he said, the assumption clear in his voice that he'd taken care of the problem. "Now when do we get our dog?" he asked.

Tom looked around at him, shook his head in wonder, and smiled. "What brought that up?"

Brian shrugged. "I just thought it was time to talk about the promise you made to get us a dog."

Tom laughed. "What kind of a dog would we be talking about here?"

"A big, black Lab!" Peter said. "Me'n Bri talked it all over, and we decided that a Lab would be best because they're real friendly and you can hunt with them. Right, Bri?"

"A male."

"On the other hand, if we got a female then we could have puppies," Tom said.

"How much do puppies sell for?" Brian asked.

Tom unfolded the newspaper, turning the pages until he reached the classified section. "Now, let's see," he ran his index finger down the page. "Well, it looks like the going price is right around four hundred."

"Dollars?" Peter asked.

"Yup," Tom said, "and if I recall right, Labs have big litters, ten, anyway. George Matterson, who lived down the road from the farm had a Lab, and she always had litters of at least ten. Once she even had twelve."

"Four thousand dollars!" Peter said.

"How do you do that?" Brian asked.

"What?"

"Multiply so fast. I couldn't even find the numbers on the calculator that fast."

"It's a trick. Dad taught me."

"Can you teach me?" He looked around at his father.

"Sure."

"When?"

"After you get back from swimming."

Brian nodded. He liked his days well ordered. "Now, about this Labrador, I..."

"Well," Tom said, "a dog like that, we'd train her to hunt. No sense having a Labrador without training it to retrieve and how to find pheasants and grouse. Peter, you're just about old enough to learn how to hunt pheasants and ducks and a Lab is the best for that sort of work."

"Okay, a female, then," Peter said.

"What does Maria want?" Tom asked.

"Lassie..." Brian said, his tone of voice making it clear that he could hardly think of a worse kind of dog to get.

"Well, now wait a minute, collies are great dogs too," Tom said. "We always had a collie around the farm and they're great dogs. None smarter than a border collie."

"Can you hunt with a collie?" Peter asked.

"No, they're mostly for herding sheep or cows. They're not hunters. But they are very smart dogs."

"Not as smart as Labs," Brian said.

"They're pretty smart, Bri," Tom said. "And if it's a border collie, they're the smartest dogs of all."

"Do border collies hunt?" Peter asked.

"No, they're strictly sheep dogs," Tom said.

"We can't get a collie," Brian said, "because if we get a collie then we'll have to start raising sheep, and we'll end up with a lot of extra chores that we have to get done everyday before we can do the things we want."

Tom laughed as Sarah walked into the kitchen. "It doesn't sound like a very serious conversation to me," she said. "Now you two go pick up your rooms, make your beds, and get changed."

They left the table and headed for the stairs, hearing their parents talking, but no longer able to make out what was being said, though they had a pretty good idea.

"Think we'll get a Lab, Peter?"

"No. Maria will get her way as usual."

"Maybe we oughta go on strike," Brian said.

"Hey! Maybe we can get two dogs! Why not? Lots of people have more than one dog. I know people who even have three dogs. Lets go for it!"

"Yeah, cool," Brian said, "two dogs would be very ultra fantastic cool."

Tom was still sitting in the kitchen when they all came back down in their bathing suits.

"Aren't you going too, Dad?" Brian asked.

"I've got to be here when the guy delivers the tractor," he said.

"A tractor! I didn't know we were getting a tractor!" Peter said.

"A real tractor?" Brian asked.

"Yup, a real tractor. Even has four wheel drive."

"Cool."

"And when you get back it'll be here, and by then I'll have it all set up and running," Tom said, as he tried to eliminate any defections from the trip to the town beach.

"Okay, guys," Sarah said. "Let's go. We still have to stop at the town hall and the MiniMart to pick up something to drink." She turned to Tom as she stepped out the door. "Have fun with your new toy," she said.

"You can count on it."

◆　◆　◆

At first they stayed together, casting occasional glances at other kids their ages, but not yet ready to take the next step. And when Peter and Brian went swimming, Maria stayed with her mother, sitting in the low slung beach chair and looking out over the sparkling pond.

"I wish we'd never moved," she said. "I miss Jen and Ann and Caitlin."

"I know," Sarah said. "It's always hard at first to make new friends, but once school starts it'll be easier."

"Didn't you move a lot when you were growing up?"

"I went to four different high schools. Grandpa kept getting transferred by the company, and every fall I had to make all new friends." She laughed. "But then when I went to college I'd had a lot of experience in making friends, so I didn't have as much trouble adjusting as kids who had always gone to the same school."

"How did you do that?"

"I just looked around till I saw someone I thought I might like, and I went up and introduced myself. It's not as hard as you think, and not once did anyone snub me. I just smiled and told them who I was, and that I was new in town. I think most kids think it's fun to meet someone new, especially if they're the first, because they get to spread the news."

"How could you be so brave? I could never do that."

Sarah smiled. "I guess you won't know that until you try, but I never thought of myself as very brave. I just wanted to have friends to make up for the ones I'd left behind, and there was only one way I knew to do that."

"Did you always move in the summer?"

"Every time. Grandpa made sure of that so we could always complete a year in the same school."

"Didn't you miss your friends?"

"Of course. But I learned, after the first time, to make new friends as soon as I could. It's funny about friends. The friendships that have lasted longest are the ones I made in college, and then after Dad and I got married."

As they talked, Maria watched a girl her age, a tall, awkward looking girl with long black hair and blue eyes, playing by the water with a boy about the same age as Brian. She thought the boy must be her brother. There was a clear resemblance. But she could also be baby-sitting him, though he seemed kind of old to need a baby-sitter.

Peter walked back up to the blanket and grabbed his towel. "What kind of a dog do you want, Maria?"

"A collie."

"What kind of collie?"

"Is there more than one?"

"Dad told us that he used to have a border collie when he was growing up on the farm in New Hampshire. He says they're the smartest dogs of all, even smarter than Labs."

She smelled a rat. Nobody talked about a dog because it was smart. They talked about what it looked like. "Do they look like a regular collie?"

Peter shrugged. "You'll have to ask Dad." He draped the towel over his shoulders. "Me'n Bri want a black Lab, so we figured the best thing was just to get two dogs and then everybody would be happy."

"Whoa, wait a minute," Sarah said. "Two dogs? Why don't

we get cats instead?"

"Because you and Dad promised we would get a dog once we moved to where we could have one. And if we get only one, then somebody's going to be unhappy, probably Maria, because Bri and me can out vote her."

"Who said anything about a vote?" Sarah asked.

"Dad said if we got a Lab then we could train it to hunt pheasants and ducks, and I could learn to hunt 'cause I'm old enough now. And we can make a lot of money too, because we could get a female, and Labs have really big litters, sometimes as many as twelve, and the puppies are worth at least four hundred dollars apiece."

"Well, before you plan too far ahead, Dad and I will need to talk this over," Sarah said. She didn't like the idea of having dogs around. They were dirty, they shed hair all over the place, and they carried fleas and ticks...and...and she had always had cats. But what she liked least was the idea of hunting. She had known it was coming, because Tom still hunted, but she had hoped he wouldn't teach the boys how to hunt. There wasn't any reason to hunt, that she could see, but she let it slide past...for now.

Peter was not backing down. "No matter what happens, though, we get at least one dog, because that was the deal."

Maria stayed out of the conversation, instead watching Brian, who had stopped near the girl and her brother and, as he usually did, had struck up a conversation. Soon enough he was down on his hands and knees helping build whatever the other boy had been working on, and that allowed her to get up, despite her fears, and walk down to look at the castle, or whatever it was. She had never done anything half so brave.

"Hi," Maria said. "I'm Maria. I see you've already met my brother Brian."

The girl smiled. "I'm Mariel and my brother's name is Tony. Are you new?"

"We moved in about a month ago."

"Are you going to the high school?"

"I'll be a freshman," Maria said.

"Oh, God, me too, and I'm scared to death." Mariel laughed and stood up, and Maria laughed with her, liking her instantly. She also liked the fact that Mariel was tall, very tall, taller than Peter by at least an inch which meant she was almost five-eleven and every bit as skinny as she was. It would be nice to finally have a tall friend, because if nothing else, it would make her feel a lot less self-conscious.

Tony looked up at the girls and then back at Brian. "You got a sister too, huh?"

"Yup."

"They're mostly a pain," he said.

"Always telling you what to do."

"Yeah, always," Tony said.

Peter didn't mind that Brian and Maria had met kids. He had too many other things to think about just now, like dogs and the new tractor, and of course the body in the bog. It was like living a mystery instead of reading one, though right now he was content just to think about it. Dad might think they had imagined the blood and the car looking like new, but they hadn't. Worse, he couldn't think of a single logical explanation. Out of the corner of his eye he saw his mother pick up a book and open it to the place she had marked, and he decided to read the book he had brought. *The Hobbit*. It was the coolest book he'd ever read. And it didn't take long to get back into it either. One paragraph and he was following Bilbo Baggins and the Dwarves and Gandalf into the Misty Mountains.

He was so absorbed by the tale that he did not see the kid

walking toward them, until out of the corner of his eye he saw a pair of large bare feet next to the edge of the blanket.

"Whatcha reading?"

Peter looked up. "*The Hobbit.*"

"I never heard of it. What's it about?"

"It's really cool. It's got dwarves and trolls and orcs and wizards and elves." He shaded his eyes against the sun. "I'm Peter," he said, "we just moved into town. Have you lived here long?"

"I was born here." He squatted down at the edge of the blanket on the sand. "My name's Mike. Where abouts do you live?"

"South County Road."

"What grade you in?"

"Seventh."

"Yeah, me too. You play sports?"

"Yup. Baseball, basketball, and soccer."

"Cool. We need some players."

"Do you play soccer or football in the fall?"

"Soccer. You said you play soccer?"

Peter nodded. "I'm a goalie."

"Cool. Our goalie stinks. He's a big fat kid and he never stops anything." Mike looked out at the pond. "You wanna go swimming? My buddies are all out on the raft."

"Sure." Peter closed his book and stood up. "I like basketball too," he said, as if either to explain or apologize for the fact that he was a good six inches taller than Mike.

"Jeesh, you're tall enough."

"I grew a lot this last year."

They started down toward the water. "My mom says I'm gonna start growing pretty soon, but so far nothing much has happened, but my father didn't get tall till he was in high school." He tossed his head in the direction of the girls. "But my sister is tall. She's gonna be at least six feet."

Sarah watched them go, delighted with her decision to get them away from the farm and...farm? Had she thought of the place as a farm? But it wasn't a farm, because nobody farmed it. Maybe buying the tractor had put that thought into her head, that and the fact that Tom had never really stopped being a farm boy. Still, she found the idea somehow upsetting. Well, perhaps not upsetting, so much as disquieting. But why? Why should that bother her? Tom hadn't said anything about raising cows or planting crops. Maybe she was just getting herself ready for the day when he did...and somehow she was sure he would.

She smiled to herself as she watched the kids. How simple they made the business of meeting people seem. And how wonderful that they had something to get their minds off that horrible story. She decided that she was angry at Mr. Barbour for having told them such a tale. Surely he had made it up. Such fantastic things just didn't happen. But making new friends would make the story less important.

She was wrong, as she found out on the ride home.

"Did you tell about the car?" Brian asked.

"We can't tell anyone else," Peter said. "No matter what happens we can't tell anybody, because the first thing you know, they'll start looking for the money."

"It's a secret," Maria said. "Our secret."

"I was gonna tell Tony about it, but I was afraid if I did the raven would get mad at us, and then some really strange stuff might happen," Brian said.

"Like what?" Maria asked.

"I don't know. I just don't want that raven mad at me."

"Maybe the raven is really the spirit of Little Louie," Maria said. "Wouldn't that be like really, really weird?"

"No. It'd be cool." Peter looked out the window. "Maybe the raven can lead us...."

"That's enough!" Sarah said. "That whole story is something Mr. Barbour made up just to scare you."

"No it isn't," Peter said. "It's true. He showed us a newspaper story about it. It was all there...well most of it anyway. But the part about Little Louie disappearing, and about how he was this terrible killer and all. That stuff was all there. And anyway, I found Hec's spent shells."

For awhile no one spoke. Then Brian broke the silence. "I was supposed to get to ride in the front," he said.

Maria groaned. "It was my turn," she said.

"No it wasn't."

"Yes it was, Bri," Peter said.

"But Maria always gets to ride in the front."

"That's not true," Maria said. "You're just trying to get Mom to feel sorry for you so you get to ride in the front. You do that all the time and you always get away with it, too. But this time I'm standing up for my rights."

"Maybe I'll get carsick and puke." Brian folded his arms across his chest and huddled down, his face pulled into a pout.

Peter laughed. "Brian Bell, the human volcano...."

"That's not funny, Peter," Sarah said. "In fact, that is particularly disgusting, and I don't want to hear anymore."

"But, Mom, he always pulls the same trick, and every time he threatens to puke you let him sit in the front seat. He's not sick, he's just making it up."

"You're such a baby, Bri," Maria said. "You always have to get your own way."

"At least I don't go around giggling about cute boys all the time," he said.

"I'm gonna kill him!" Maria shouted. "I'm not even gonna wait till we get home. You little nerd, you're nothing but a dweeb with his nose in the books all the time, always kissing up to your teachers."

"Maria! That's enough. If I hear you say anything like that again, I'll ground you for the summer. And that goes for you too, Brian. I have absolutely had it with you guys fighting over every little tiny, stupid thing. Sometimes I think we should put you all in cages in the backyard."

"I wasn't really gonna kill him, Mom, honest. I was just gonna torture him a little."

"Maria! That's enough!"

Peter sat with his arms folded over his chest, delighted that he had somehow managed to keep out of it. But it helped that he had only one thing on his mind, and it wasn't the tractor. He was certain that the money was still there somewhere, and he was equally sure it wasn't in the bog. He had no reason to believe that, but he believed it anyway. The only thing stopping him from looking was the blood they had seen in the car, and the notion that the raven might really be Little Louie's spirit. Somehow, he would have to get over that, because it was absolutely clear that he was going to go look for that money whether Maria and Brian came with him or not, though he thought he would feel a lot safer if they did. Sometimes Maria understood stuff that other people didn't, and Brian had other kinds of answers. What I do best, he thought, is put things logically. Together, we make a great team and that's pretty weird when you think about how much fighting we do. But fighting doesn't really mean anything. It's just something brothers and sisters do.

Chapter Six

Some Surprises

But what they found when they got home blew Peter's plans to smithereens, for there, sitting in the barn, was the purple car. It had been put up on concrete blocks and the wheels were off and the hood was up, and Tom was leaning so far in over the engine that you could only see his legs and his rear end. It looked as if the car had opened its hood by itself and decided to swallow him.

Hearing the car on the gravel drive, he pulled himself from under the hood, and as he wiped his hands on a grease rag, walked out to meet them.

"Now, how's this for a surprise? I was trying out the tractor and I decided I'd put it to good use and tow the car in so I could restore it. Apart from the bullet holes, it's in amazingly good shape. There's some rust, but nothing I can't fix."

Maria, Peter, and Brian stood with mouths open, staring at the car. Sarah had never gotten used to the idea that her husband could fix things. "What on earth are you going to do with it? It's just an old piece of junk?"

"Sarah, this is a great find. It's in wonderful shape. I've got the tools I need, and I ought to be able to finish before winter. There's just not a whole lot wrong with it." Tom went on talking, never for a second thinking that anyone would disagree with what he had done. "I also talked to a history professor over at the university, and he filled me in on Little Louie LaMontaigne. It seems he was one of the most famous hired killers in the country. In fact..." he turned and swept his arm toward the car, "this car is a part of American history! I'm gonna restore it to showroom condition, all except for the bullet holes and the bloodstain. It could be worth thirty thousand bucks!"

Peter walked into the barn and looked carefully at the car, walking around it, running his hand over the cool surface. It didn't look like the same car sitting here in the barn. It just looked like some old car that somebody was getting ready to fix up. There was nothing weird or spooky about it. Then he looked at the old stain on the back of the driver's seat.

"Little Louie," Tom said, "killed over a hundred men, according to Professor Batchelder."

"Did he know about what happened here?" Maria asked.

"All he knew was what the newspapers said, and that wasn't anywhere near as much as Walt told us. In fact he's going to call Walt and make an appointment to see him so he can get the rest of the story."

"Did he say anymore about the search for the body?" Brian

asked, firing his question in machine gun fashion.

"Nothing beyond what Walt told us."

Maria stood just outside the barn. "Do you think the body's still there?"

"Just the bones," Brian said. "I told you the eels and the turtles would have taken care of everything else."

"Turtles! You never told me about turtles!" Maria looked anxiously at Sarah. "Turtles eat bodies? I thought they just ate bugs and stuff."

"Snapping turtles eat anything they can find or catch," Brian said. So did the other turtles, but he decided not to mention that. Maria would never go swimming again.

Maria glanced down at the water, rippling in the sunlight. "Do we have any snapping turtles in our pond?"

"Jeez," Peter said. "Wake up and smell the coffee, Maria, Bri already told us all about this stuff."

"Every pond has snappers," Tom said. "But you don't have to worry about them. They hide deep in the mud."

"Oh, that's just great," Maria said. "And what happens when you step on them?"

"Maria," Peter said, "how much time do you spend walking in the mud?"

"Ugh! Never. I hate mud. But even more I hate the thought of turtles eating bodies. It's the grossest thing I ever heard."

"What's gross about that?" Brian looked up at his tall, slender sister, wondering if there would ever come a time when he understood girls. Probably not. How could you understand anyone who was afraid of snakes and bugs and turtles and frogs and didn't eat meat? Even harder to understand, was how she went all wild over some freako rock and roll band. But then the girls his age weren't much different. All they ever talked about was clothes, boys, and the latest bands.

Peter walked back to the open door of the barn and stood looking at the car. "Are you gonna paint it the same color?"

"Absolutely. I'm gonna make it look just the way it did when it was sitting in the showroom in 1940...a beautiful glossy black, so shiny it'll hurt your eyes to look at it."

"But...but it's purple," Maria said.

It only looks purple because of the way the paint has oxidized from sitting outside for fifty-five years," Tom said. "If you look under the hood where the paint was protected from the weather, you can see the original color."

They all trooped over to look.

"Gee," Brian said, "As much as I hate the color purple, I think I like it better than black."

"Me too," Maria said.

"It's a whole lot spookier," Peter said.

"Very spooky..." Brian rolled his eyes upward.

"But it *will* look beautiful when it's finished," Maria said.

"And the bullet holes and the bloodstain will still be there," Peter said.

"So it'll look just like it did the day Little Louie got machine-gunned by the gang. Cool," Brian said.

Sarah shivered. "That doesn't sound so cool to me, but then I never did hold with machine-gunnings. I don't even like movies that have that kind of thing in them. And didn't Hec Chandler say the car was jinxed?"

Tom grinned. "That's what Walt said, but what he didn't say was what made Hec think that. Sometimes those old timers got a thing into their heads, and they just believed it whether there was any truth to it or not. Old Parker Carleton up home believed that you couldn't kill a deer on an east wind so he never hunted on an east wind. And then when I was twelve, I went out to hunt on an east wind and shot the biggest buck I'd ever seen, and when Dad told Parker about it, he just shrugged and said the wind must have been shifting around."

Sarah watched her kids carefully. Diversion was not working. All three were focused on the car and could not be lured to other lines of thought.

"It'll be really cool, Dad," Peter said," all shiny just like a new car. Do you think it'll run?"

"If it won't, I'll fix it."

"You can fix cars?" Maria asked.

"I'm a mechanical engineer, remember."

"But you go to work in a suit and tie? Guys who fix cars wear uniforms that have their name over the pocket, and you went to college, and those guys haven't been to college."

Tom grinned. "But they could have gone. A lot of mechanics are smart enough to go. But they just aren't interested. The difference is, Maria, that while I like to fix things, I wanted to know how to make them, and for that you need to study engineering. Not to make one thing, but to figure out how to make millions of them all the same. What I do is design machines to manufacture parts."

Brian looked up at his father, surprised that until this second he had not known what his father did every day. Designing machines...just what, he wondered, did that mean? And what the heck was a machine anyway?

Peter cut to the chase. "Can we drive it?"

Tom looked down at Peter. "Well, you're tall enough now, and I sure don't plan to sell it right away."

"I can drive it," Maria said. "And in two years I'll have my license." It delighted her to watch her brothers squirm with envy. They deserved it. Maybe if they hadn't acted so superior about snakes and turtles, she'd have gone easy on them. No. You didn't pass up a chance like this.

Tom tried to shift the subject before another minor word war broke out. "I'm going to have a bronze plaque made, and I'll mount it on the passenger side door so people can read about what happened."

No reaction. They were absolutely fixated on the car. He reached into his shirt pocket and took out a celluloid folder. "I found this in the glove compartment after I picked the lock." He held it out so they all could read it. "Can you imagine? There he was, with half the law officers in the country looking for him, number one on the FBI's most wanted list, and...."

"You can pick a lock?" It was Sarah's turn to look surprised. "I thought only burglars and crooks did that."

"It's easy enough, once you know what a lock looks like inside." He turned back to the kids. "So he waltzes into a Motor Vehicle Department office and registers the car in his own name." He pointed to the name. "Louis Francis Xavier LaMontaigne. Can you imagine the brass of the man?"

"Talk about guts," Peter said.

"But who would have been looking for anyone with that name?" Sarah asked. "And after all, there are a lot of LaMontaignes around here. Just look in the phone book."

"You got that right," Tom said. "And what's more, Little Louie was a true master of disguise. Professor Batchelder told me that he once dressed up as a rag picker, and when he knocked on his mother's door, she didn't recognize him."

"Wow, cool," Peter said.

"And just what is this project likely to cost?" Sarah asked.

Tom shrugged. "Oh, a couple of thousand maybe. I won't know until I get to work on the engine. The parts can be pretty pricey for these old cars, but at least I don't have to hire a mechanic or a body man either, for that matter."

"Tom, we don't have that kind of money. We need a new refrigerator and a dishwasher and..."

"Not all at once, Sarah. One piece here, another piece there...but mostly it'll be a lot of work. I'll do the body work and the upholstery. The tires will be expensive, but not much more than the tires we put on our cars now."

He walked over to her. "I'm going in for a cup of coffee," he said as he wrapped his arm around her shoulders and steered her toward the house. "Look, you grew up in a place where men played golf and bridge. I grew up in the country where if you wanted something fixed, you fixed it."

"You think she'll go for it?" Peter asked.

"I don't know," Maria said as she shook her head slowly form side to side. "We really do need a new dishwasher and a new refrigerator."

"Maybe," Peter said, "we could all do dishes at night, and on the weekends Mom could do the others."

"I pretty much hate doing dishes," Brian said.

"Me too, Bri," Peter said, "but sometimes you have to make sacrifices to get what you want."

"Like you've ever made a sacrifice," Maria said.

Peter grinned. "I've made lots of sacrifices. This past spring I made three of them and each time I got the runner into scoring position."

"What are you talking about?" Maria asked.

"Baseball," Brian said. "Sacrifice bunts."

"What's a bunt?"

"Do you really not know what a bunt is?" Peter asked.

"Never mind that," Brian said. "What we need to do is go find Little Louie's million dollars."

"Okay," Maria said. "When do we start?"

"I think tomorrow morning," Peter said.

"But we have to steer clear of the bog," Brian said. "I read up on 'em just to be sure. They are truly nasty."

"We will," Peter said. "Well, we might have to go down to the edge of it and look around to see whether Little Louie went out onto it or not."

Tom came back out carrying his cup of coffee. "Didn't you guys tell me that you saw a raven?"

"Yeah," Peter said. "Bri spotted it. I thought it was just a big crow."

"Well that's another thing Professor Batchelder told me. Little Louie had a sort of code name among the criminals. He was known as...*THE RAVEN*...."

Maria, Peter, and Brian looked as if someone had just poured buckets of ice water over their heads.

Chapter Seven

The Trail Grows Warm

On Sunday, while Tom was busy working on the car and Sarah had taken the overgrown perennial gardens to task, Maria, Peter, and Brian hiked out across the field to where the car had sat nestled into the brush beneath the trees.

"Didn't Mr. Barbour say the cars were out in the field when the shooting started?" Peter asked.

Maria nodded.

"What I thought was maybe we could find the old cartridge cases." Peter looked out at the field.

"Why would we want the cartridge cases?" Brian asked.

"What good are old cartridge cases?" Maria asked.

"Because if we could figure out where the Cadillac was,

we could figure out where the Ford was, and then we'd be able to figure out which way Little Louie went. And if we knew that, then we'd know where he went out onto the bog. And if we knew that, we could sight out over the bog, and maybe figure out whether he could have hidden out there."

"Forty-five caliber." Brian said, his voice very even and low, the way it always was when he had information to deliver. "Machine guns are forty-five caliber." He looked out over the field. "Probably buried."

"Why would they be buried?" Peter asked.

"Dust and pieces of hay and leaves break down into dirt. That's how we get topsoil." Brian looked up at his brother. "Don't you guys read anything interesting?"

"If I wanted to be an encyclopedia, I'd move into my bookcase," Maria said. "And anyway, science is all about creepy gross stuff that makes me want to puke."

"Like boys...." Brian said.

"Bri, you are such a nerd."

"What you need, Maria, is an air valve in your ear so you could get a refill from the compressor in the barn, instead of having to depend on osmosis," Brian said.

"That just proves it," Maria said. "Only a nerd would even know what a word like osmosis means."

"We could use the metal detector," Peter said, as he tried to break up the bickering before it blew up into a boxing match.

Maria looked back toward the barren, dead, gray rectangle where the car had sat for even more years than her father had been alive, and then looked out across the field and the heat waves dancing in the sun. "How far out would you guess?"

"Where did you find the shells, Peter?" Brian asked.

"On that high point," Peter said, "I marked it in three directions."

Brian looked around at his older brother, brushing back his blond hair. "When did you get so smart," he said.

"I do the practical stuff, Bri, that's what I'm good at. That and math, and one day I'm gonna be an engineer like dad. But the genius stuff is your department."

"Good old Brian." Maria reached out and ran her hand through his thick hair."

"Hey, don't do that!" He ducked away. "Only little kids like stuff like that." But it wasn't true, he thought. He did like it when Maria touched his hair, though for the life of him, he couldn't think why.

"None of this makes any difference," Maria said. "We know he went to the bog, because the dogs tracked him there, right?" She pointed to a place at the opposite corner of the field. "Look. There. See where you can see the sky through the trees? It has to be there, and he must have headed for it."

"How would he have known it was there?" Peter asked.

"The same way I did," Maria said. "He probably was afraid of the woods, and he headed for the most light."

"But why?" Peter stuffed his hands into the pockets of his shorts. "It's all open. Wouldn't he have been looking for a place to hide? You can't hide in the open."

"Maybe he guessed they'd get the bloodhounds, and he wanted to get into the water to throw them off," Brian said.

"That makes sense," Maria said.

"Let's go." Peter stepped out into the field. "Last one there is a maggot covered road kill."

"Oh, gross, Peter." Maria began to run. She quickly passed Peter, her long legs carrying her along effortlessly. At times she seemed to float above the ground, her long hair flying out behind.

One day, Peter thought, as he tried in vain to catch her, one day I'll be strong enough, but even as he thought it, he doubted it. The fact was that Maria could run like a rabbit, and at their old school she had broken nearly every record for both the boy's and the girl's track teams.

As usual, Brian brought up the rear, though this time that didn't worry him, because just now getting to the bog first was nowhere near as important as getting there last. He saw the raven watching them from high up in the big old pumpkin pine at the edge of the field. So far the bird had been quiet and Brian wondered if that was why neither Maria nor Peter had spotted him. For now that was just as well, because, even if he hated to admit it, that bird was very, very spooky.

He had expected them to go charging off into the woods, but instead they stopped near the edge of the field, and he caught up. The trees grew thick there, the trunks close together, and only a short way in, a stand of young pine blocked their way. There seemed to be no easy way in, and they walked along the edge until they came to a narrow path. Still they held back, as fantastic cartoon visions of forests rose in their imaginations, tree branches becoming the arms of vicious tree beings that sent their roots slithering like fat dark snakes across the path, waiting to wrap around their legs and draw them down into the dark earth.

"Who made this path?" Maria asked.

Peter shrugged. "Hikers? Hikers make a lot of trails."

Brian shook his head. "Deer," he said as he aimed his index finger at an indentation in the soft earth where the path began. "There's a track," he said. "The deer come out and feed in the field, and then they go back into the woods and down to the bog for water, and then probably into those hemlocks over there to sleep." He looked up at Peter. "I got a whole book on tracks. Grandpa gave it to me for Christmas, and he took me outside to show me the tracks in the snow."

"Why didn't he show us?" Peter asked.

"Because you were busy playing Gameboy, and Maria was reading and didn't want to go out 'cause it was cold'. I can tell otter tracks too and beaver and fox and deer mice, and...."

"Okay, Bri, we got it," Peter said. "The question is whether we'll get lost if we follow the path."

"Jeez, Peter," Brian shook his head. "We're only going to the bog. You don't even need a path for that. You can see it." Feeling quite full of himself after having shown up his brother and sister, Brian walked into the woods.

This time Peter and Maria were left to follow, and Brian liked that even better. Served them right for all the times he'd ended up running his legs off trying to catch up to them. And there was nothing to be afraid of in the woods. It was safer than any city street, and this far south they didn't even have bears. Not that bears were a problem, because black bears always ran off. He and Grandpa and Dad had surprised one in the raspberries last summer at the farm, and all the bear did was snort and run off.

Within seconds they were standing at the edge of the bog, looking out across the low tangle of vegetation toward the water nearly a hundred yards from shore. Here and there near the edges of the bog, the soft silver trunks of long dead trees poked up through the plants and bushes.

"This place gives me the creeps." Maria wrapped her arms around herself to control a deep shiver. "It looks like no one has ever been here."

"The Creature from the Black Lagoon could come out of a place like this," Peter said. "Look at all those dead trees.

What do you think could have killed so many of them?"

As usual, Brian saw it differently. But then he liked swamps and bogs because they were full of frogs and turtles and birds and stuff you never saw in other places. "Cool," Brian said. "This is a real bog, not just a swamp. All those bushes are floating on the water. That's why it's so danger- ous. It looks like solid ground, but you can go right through, and you can't tell how deep the water is underneath."

"I think I liked it much better in the field," Maria said. "Maybe we ought to go back and get the metal detector so we can look for those, those, whatever you called those things."

"Good idea," Peter said.

"Why?" Brian asked.

"We were told to stay away from here," Maria said.

"But it's okay if you stay on the edge." Brian pointed to a path that followed along the bog. "That's what the deer do. They know where it's safe. They don't walk onto the bog because they know what can happen."

"How would they know that? Deer can't think," Maria said. "If it's one thing I did learn in science, it's that only humans can think."

"The way it works," Brian said, "is that the fawns walk where their mothers take them, and that way they learn the safe paths. This path was probably here when Little Louie was gunned down."

Maria got it. "Because each new generation of deer learns from their parents. That's a pretty neat concept, Bri." She smiled. "Maybe science isn't so bad after all."

"As long as nothing happens to make them change, they'll just keep using the same trails over and over," Brian said.

"Listen," Maria said. "We followed one of those paths from the field, and maybe that was because it was the easiest way, or maybe because we thought it was safer to follow a path than just cut through the woods."

"So?" Peter looked puzzled as he often did when trying to follow Maria's logic.

"So...Little Louie lived in the city. He would probably have done the same thing." She saw something shiny out of the corner of her eye and glanced down at Brian's right sneaker. "Bri, what's that on your Nike?"

Both boys looked down.

Suddenly Maria looked very pale. "Oh my God...."

"It looks like blood," Brian said. He squatted down on his haunches to get a better look. "Yup. Blood. No doubt about it." He smeared it with his finger. "Yeah, that's blood all right." He stood up and held his finger so he could get a better look, and then stuck the finger out toward Maria and Peter. "Just what I said. Blood. Fresh, and plenty of it too."

"Maybe you cut yourself," Peter said.

Brian looked at his arms, exposed below his tee shirt, and then down at his legs below his shorts, but he saw no cuts. "Nope, no cuts that I can see."

"Look! There..." Maria pointed to the laurel branches which swept into the path. "There's more of it!"

"Wow, cool," Peter said as he looked at the blood, and then let his eye follow the path along the bog. "Hey, there's more over there, and I think there's more up ahead. Com'on, we gotta check this out."

"Not me!" Maria shouted. "I am absolutely out of here and I am never coming back...I am never coming anywhere near this place again." She turned and ran up the path to the field, not looking back, and not stopping even when she ran out into the open.

"Do you think it really is blood, like the stuff on the seat?"

Brian asked.

"Sure," Peter said. "And I'll tell you what else I think. I think it's Little Louie's blood."

Slowly they started along the path by the bog, pushing aside the branches from the hemlocks and alders. They found spots of blood on the ground, lying atop the dead leaves and needles, and they found other patches on the green leaves of the brush, most of then at the height of Peter's stomach.

"I never saw such bright blood," Peter said.

"Artery blood. Little Louie must have got shot through the chest."

"Then he must have been really short if his chest only came up to my stomach." He stopped and straightened up, slowly looking around. "Whoa. Wait a minute. This is crazy! Here we are following a blood trail left by a man over fifty years ago. There has to be another way to explain this. Maybe somebody shot a deer or a...a, com'on, Bri, give me some help here. What else could a hunter have shot."

"Only a deer would be tall enough to leave blood that high. But it would have to be a poacher, because deer season isn't open. This blood is so fresh we'd have heard the shot."

"Brian! Peter!" Maria called from the field. "Are you coming or not?"

"Just a minute, Maria!" Peter called back. "We'll be there in just a minute!"

"Maybe it isn't blood," Brian said.

"Then what is it?"

"I don't know. But it couldn't be blood...could it?"

"I don't like this, Bri, it's making me pretty nervous."

Suddenly the raven began to rattle at them.

"He sounds human," Peter said.

"They can be trained to talk, just like crows. I wish I'd

listened better to the ravens. Then I'd know if this one sounded any different. I think he does, but I can't be sure."

Suddenly the bird made a sound they had not heard before, a strange garbled noise that sounded very human.

CLDNDLNLYBVDGRND
BRYDBNSNDDTRZRBFND....

Then it repeated the call again...louder this time, the sound ringing out through the woods. But unlike other bird calls which usually taper off, this seemed to get louder.

CLDNDLNLYBVDGRND
BRYDBNSNDDTRZRBFND....

"What the heck was that?" Peter said. "It sounds almost like words."

"Pretty crazy words," Brian said. "But it doesn't sound like any raven I remember from the farm."

The raven called again, the strange collection of sounds ringing through the silent summer air, rattling off the trunks of the trees. Each time the bird repeated a phrase the sound came louder and louder, and the effect on Brian and Peter was immediate. It spooked them thoroughly and completely, sending shivers right down to the soles of their feet. And then they ran, ran just as fast as they could, ignoring the path, and cutting uphill through the woods, fending off the brush with their hands and arms, willingly absorbing the punishment of the branches whipping their arms and legs rather than stay a second longer in those woods.

Chapter Eight

A Voice on the Wind

Drawn by the noises in the garage, Peter and Brian followed the sounds across the yard to the open door. Maria sat on a stool just inside, watching Tom working on the engine of the Purple Car. The seats had been taken out and set to the side, the inside of the car shone, and any rusty metal had been sanded, buffed, and repainted with primer.

Tom looked around at the boys as they walked into the garage. "You wouldn't believe what dynamite shape this car is in," he said. "I don't even believe what good shape it's in. No rust inside at all. The gas tank is sound and the gaskets on the engine are okay. I already pulled the head and checked them, and, in fact, I was just about to try turning it over."

"Turning it over!" Brian said. "Why would you do that?"
Tom looked over at Brian, not sure just how to answer.
Peter laughed. "He means he's going to try starting the engine. It doesn't mean he's going to turn the whole car upside down." Peter made a circular motion with his hand. "Turning it over means getting the starter to make the inside of the engine go around."

"Jeez, Peter," Brian said. "I got it, okay? I'm not dumb."
Maria laughed. "I liked the idea of turning it upside down. Maybe we could shake out the spooks."

Tom ignored the remark. "Did you know the key was still in the ignition? I lubricated the lock with graphite, put in a new battery, checked the wiring, and it was perfect. It's absolutely unbelievable that the mice hadn't chewed the wiring out of it. That's what usually happens when you leave a car sitting for any length of time." He reached into the car, shifting the transmission to neutral. "Now comes the acid test. Will it run?" He turned the key, pushed the starter button, and the engine turned over, slowly at first, grinding and grinding, and then gradually grinding faster and faster, then it sputtered, threw a great cloud of blue smoke out the tailpipe, almost caught, sputtered once more, and died.

"Whoa," Peter said. "Check out the smoke."

Maria and Brian started coughing and waving their hands past their faces to clear the air. Tom ignored them as he pushed the starter again. The result was the same, nothing but noise and a lot more smoke, so thick that it sent the kids scurrying out of the barn. He stood back and scratched his head. "It should start. I replaced all the parts, I cleaned and drained the gas tank, and put in new gas. Maybe I left too much oil in the cylinders." He crossed his arms over his chest. "Maybe I ought to replace the rings and grind the valves." He shook his head.

"Naw, that can't be it. The car has less than a hundred miles on it and there wasn't even any rust in the cylinders." He looked up suddenly. "Pretty darn peculiar, I'd say. Those cylinders should've been solid with rust, but even before I oiled it, I could turn the flywheel, and that was very strange."

"Everything about this is strange." Maria stepped back into the barn, followed by her brothers.

"What will it take to get it running?" Peter asked. He glanced at Maria quickly, hoping she'd understand and shut up. Sometimes Maria talked too much.

"No idea," Tom said. "I'll just have to go through it all from the beginning till I find out where I made my mistake. I could have set the timing wrong, used the wrong gap on the plugs, any one of a number of things." He picked up a rag and began wiping the grease from his hands. "But that's what makes working on old cars fun. You never know what little thing you've overlooked until you find it."

Brian, his hands stuffed into the pockets of his shorts, sauntered up and looked into the engine well. He shook his head and clicked his tongue. "Probably won't run until we take care of Little Louie's ghost," he said.

"What?" Tom burst out laughing. "Little Louie's ghost?"

"Sure," Brian said, ignoring the strained looks from his brother and sister. "The way I figure it, Little Louie died some-where around here and never got buried, and I've read that when a thing like that happens the spirit roams free until the body gets laid to rest. Spirits like that can get into all kinds of mischief, and sometimes they're pretty mean and evil, and can cause people to go insane."

"So," Tom said, "you think that the trouble with this en-gine is Little Louie LaMontaigne's ghost, which somehow is keeping it from running, and no matter what I do, even if I restore this engine to brand new, it still won't run."

Brian nodded. "That's just the way it is, Dad. I know it's pretty hard to accept stuff like that, but, hey, sometimes you have to adjust."

Tom nearly fell over. How many times had he used those very words in trying to get them past some disappointment? But it wasn't just the words, it was the way Brian delivered them. Tom shook his head. "I think you guys ought to try thinking about something else. This is getting a little wild."

Peter reacted quickly. "Hey, how about we go look for the old cartridge casings. All we need is the metal detector."

"That's a great idea. Why don't you do that? We'll make them part of the display. It's in the front hall closet. You'll have to put a new battery in it."

"Nine volt?"

"Yup," Tom said. "There are two new ones in the bottom drawer in the island in the kitchen." He tossed the grease rag onto the work bench. "Do you know where to start looking?"

"I don't know," Peter said, "maybe a hundred and fifty yards from where I found those other cases."

"Good thinking."

"Maria, you get the battery and I'll get the detector," Peter said as they turned toward the house.

"No. I'll get the detector and you get the battery," Maria said, for no other reason than to make sure he understood he was not giving the orders.

"Whatever. I don't care, just get going."

They rendezvoused back in the kitchen, but Maria wanted no part of going anywhere near where they had been.

"Com'on, Maria," Peter said, "we won't even be close to the woods." He popped open the battery compartment of the metal detector, removed the old battery, and handed it to Brian who stuck it into the battery tester. "And besides, who knows what we might find."

She shook her head. "I'm not going out there ever again." But even as she said it, she knew she would. She had to. She had to know what was out there, and she had to know what the raven was saying, even if it wasn't really saying anything.

"This battery's flat as a fart," Brian said as he dropped it into the trash can and looked at Maria. "There's nothing to be scared of," he said.

"Right, Bri. God, you even had the blood on you."

"But it's gone now. It went away when I stepped into the field."

"See, Maria? The scary stuff only happens in the woods." Peter slipped the new battery into the compartment, slid the cover back into place, and turned on the switch. The green light on the console box came on, and the machine began to hum softly.

"I'm not going." She walked across the kitchen, pulled a chair out from the table, and sat down, staring out the window toward the pond.

Peter looked at her more carefully. "I'm starting to think you really are scared."

"What I don't understand is why you two aren't."

Peter shrugged. "I don't know either. I'm just not."

"Maybe you don't know enough about ghosts."

"Yeah, right. Just 'cause you're older, you think you know everything."

"Blow it out your nose, Peter. You never read anything. What do you know about ghosts."

"Ghosts can be simply mischievous or they can be truly evil," Brian said as he launched into another of his lectures. "There have been any number of cases where their antics, even harmless stuff, led people into doing things they wouldn't have done otherwise. Most ghosts, or so some people believe, merely reflect the character of the person they once were. Someone who was evil will be evil as a ghost, and someone who was good is likely to be playful. There was a case once in Kentucky of a man who was hanged for murder, but instead of burying him the people were so angry they let him rot until only his bones hung from the tree, and then they scattered the bones far and wide.

"Those who saw the ghost only ever saw a few bones at a time, and they believed he was searching for the rest of his skeleton, and that sometimes he killed people for their bones. They found several dead people over the years who were missing various bones."

Maria groaned. "Oh great, Bri. That helped a lot. Now I'm hardly scared at all. Every time I go out there, I'll be perfectly calm thinking about how I might lose my bones."

"I knew you wanted to go," Peter said.

"I didn't say that!"

"Yes you did."

"I figure," Brian said, "that if we find Little Louie's bones and then bury them he'll disappear."

Maria shivered. "Bri, you are really losing it. You actually want to go looking for his bones? Do you know how crazy that is? God, Bri, that is totally, like, spastic."

"But we can't do it without your help," He said. "One of the books I read says that sometimes girls your age can hear spirits, but boys can't hear them at all. It'd be a big help if we knew just what Little Louie wanted us to do."

"Another comforting thought," Maria said. "Just what I always wanted, a good old heart-to-heart talk with a ghost." But she could feel her curiosity rising like a stream in a heavy rain, rising right to the edge of her common sense and threatening to overflow. Did she really believe in ghosts? Of course not! There was always some logical explanation for even the strangest stuff. There was even an explanation for the blood. They just hadn't figured it out yet.

"Okay," she said, "I'll go, but I'm not going into those woods and I'm not going near the bog."

With the metal detector in hand, they trooped out into the middle of the field and began looking for the shell casings. Peter set the machine to its most sensitive level, and nestled the head of the detector into the lush green grass, noticing for the first time how long the grass had gotten since they moved in. "Can you believe how much this grass has grown," he said. "I'm just glad I don't have to mow this too. It takes me half-a-day now to cut the lawn."

"It wouldn't take long with the new tractor," Brian said.

"That'd be cool," Peter said. "In fact that would be awesome!" He looked around, his eyes drifting over the field. "But it's still pretty big, Bri."

Peter switched on the machine and they started where they thought the second car had stopped, and then worked back and forth, all of them tense as they waited for the needle to jump and the sound level to rise suddenly. But after several passes, the job seemed hopeless. The field was just too big, and the soft green grass seemed to stretch on forever.

"Maybe you're not doing it right," Brian said.

"Of course I'm doing it right. What kind of a doofus do you think I am?"

"A dorky doofus," Brian said.

Maria laughed. "Really cool move there, Bro. Talk about wide open. You're gonna have to get your act together before you start seventh grade or the cool people will eat you alive and you'll wind up hanging out with all the dorks."

"If the cool people are like the dickheads you used to hang with, then I'd rather hang with the dorks," Peter shot back. "And anyway, I'll be playing basketball and baseball and soccer, and jocks are never dorks."

"Oh, wow, am I impressed or what?" She stopped and leaned on the long handle of the shovel. "Hey, how come I get to carry the shovel?"

"Cause men know how to run machines," he said, knowing an explosion would follow and watching her out of the corner of his eye to make sure she didn't come after him with the shovel. She had a wild temper. But instead, she sat down in the field, her arms supporting her from behind as she closed her eyes and raised her face toward the sun. "Call me if you find anything," she said. "I'm going to work on my tan."

"You're not supposed to do that anymore," Brian said. "Too many holes in the ozone. You'll get skin cancer."

"How can the sun be good for everything else and bad for people?" Maria said. "Can you answer that? All I hear is, 'sun will cause skin cancer.' And then I read that if you don't get enough sun, you won't get enough vitamin D, but nobody says how much is too much or how much is enough."

Brian shook his head. There had to be a reason. It was only a matter of finding it, but right now he had other things on his mind. He stayed close to Peter, watching the needle as they drifted slowly back and forth across the imaginary line they had drawn toward where the car had sat in the woods. How could Maria find this boring? Sooner or later the needle was bound to jump. You just had to have faith.

Maria turned her face away from the sun and watched her brothers. This was much better than wandering around in circles, much...she felt something crawling on her leg and looked down to see a tiny spider foraging across her knee-cap. "A SPIDER! OH, GOD! A SPIDER ON MY LEG!" She began jumping up and down. "I hate SPIDERS! Spiders? There are spiders out here! Did I know there were spiders out here? No, of course I didn't know there were spiders out here! And why didn't I know there were spiders out here? I didn't know because nobody told me there were spiders out here, especially my little spastic brother who knows all about everything, and didn't tell me there were spiders out here, and now I'm absolutely stuck in the middle of spider heaven, and I'm going to have to hit someone!"

Peter and Brian turned to watch. "She's afraid of spiders," Brian said, shaking his head. How could anyone be afraid of spiders? For that matter, how could anyone be afraid of half the things Maria was afraid of. In fact the only thing she wasn't afraid of was teenage boys, and it didn't take a lot of brains to figure out that they were truly dangerous.

"Yup," Peter said, "she's afraid of spiders all right." As he watched Maria, he swung the metal detector without thinking about it, and suddenly the steady drone pitched upward and the needle shot to the right.

"Hey!" Brian shouted, "Hey, there's something here!"

Peter swung the detector slowly back and forth until the high pitched hum steadied out. "I got it. It's right under here. Maria! Bring the shovel."

The excitement proved just strong enough to overcome the spiders, and she grabbed the shovel and ran through the field. Without hesitating, she plunged the shovel blade into the ground, jumped with both feet onto the back of the blade, and drove it into the soil. With the first shovelful, they dropped onto their knees and began breaking the turf apart, searching for the piece of metal which had set off the detector.

Suddenly Maria looked up. "Did you hear that?"

"Hear what?" Peter asked.

"A voice. I heard a voice."

"I told you," Brian said, "girls hear this stuff."

"What did it say?" Peter glanced uneasily toward the bog.

"Quiet...." She sat back onto her legs folded beneath her, listening, but the sound did not come again and she shook her head. "Maybe it was the wind," she said.

"Did it say anything?" Peter asked.

"I'm not sure. I wasn't listening and then all of a sudden I heard a voice, a man's voice. I think it was a man's voice."

"Shucks," Brian said, holding up an old rusted nail. "It was only a nail." He reached back into the dirt, picked up an iron ring about two inches in diameter and held it up.

"Wait!" Maria shouted. "He's talking again! I can hear him. Listen...." She stood quietly looking off toward the woods at the end of the field above the bog. "I'm dying," she said.

"What!" Peter looked genuinely alarmed.

"No. Not me! That's what the voice said."

Brian stared at her. "It's Little Louie! Keep listening!"

In the middle of the field, sweating in the hot sun, they waited, but the voice did not come again. The strangest thing, Maria thought, was that she wasn't the least bit scared. In fact the spider had scared her more. So had the blood. On the other hand both of those had been real, and this she still couldn't be sure about. Maybe it had been a voice, maybe it had been the wind. No, she thought, it was a voice, a strange, high voice, and the words had been absolutely clear. Now they had to find out what those words meant.

Chapter Nine

The Bog Beckons

The detector sounded again and Brian grabbed the shovel, dug out two clumps of turf, squatted down, and began pulling one of the clumps apart. Peter dropped onto his knees and attacked the second clump, pulling and tearing, shaking the dirt from the matted roots as he watched for any sign of metal.

Not until Brian stood up to dig another clump of sod did Peter look around for Maria, and when he didn't see her, he thought she must have gone back to the house. He stood up and shaded his eyes against the sun, but all he could see was the field rolling back toward the house. He turned slowly, wondering where she had gone, because he was certain she hadn't had time to get back to the house, and then he saw her, walking away from them, walking straight toward the end of the field and the path to the bog.

"Maria! Hey, Maria. Where are you going?" he called. But she did not seem to hear him so he shouted again, louder this time. "Maria, where are you going?"

Why didn't she answer? And why was she walking so weird, stiff, like a zombie. "Bri," he said, "I think there's something wrong with Maria."

"Hey, look at this!" Brian shouted as he held up an old tarnished forty-five caliber cartridge case. "I found one."

"Never mind that! There's something wrong with Maria. Look at her. She's walking like she's in a trance of some kind. Com'on, Bri. Run! We've got to help her. We've got to stop her. She's headed for the bog!"

They ran as fast as they could through the ankle deep grass, getting ahead of her just as she entered the woods.

Peter, panting and out of breath, walked backward in front of her, glancing over his shoulder to make sure he stayed on the path, and all the while talking to her, his voice, betraying his fear with it's high whining pitch. "Maria? What's the matter, Maria? Stop! Listen to me! Can you hear me?"

She did not stop, and if she heard him she showed no sign. Her eyes glazed and focused far away, looked through him.

"Maria! Maria!" he shouted. "Snap out of it!"

On she went, staring ahead toward the bog below.

"What do I do, Bri?" Peter called. "What should I do? Think of something, Bri, think of something quick, because I can't stop her."

"I don't know. Just stop her!"

He grabbed her shoulders and tried to turn her, but she simply swept him out of her way, knocking him into the brush as if he were nothing more than a pesky fly.

"What the hell!" Peter shouted as he pulled himself out of a patch of laurel. "What the hell is going on here?"

Brian ran on ahead, picking up a dead oak branch, and when Maria came past, he stuck the branch between her legs. But she walked right through it, snapping the stout branch as if it were a piece of the balsa wood he used to make his model planes. On she walked, straight down the path, straight for the bog, her brothers running after her, helpless, panicked, pleading with her to stop. But she did not stop, and when she reached the bog, she simply walked out onto the thick mat, her feet finding their way through the dense cover without a single misstep as she moved farther and farther from shore.

With each step they waited for her to fall through into the dark water below, but she just walked across the top of the bog toward what looked like a small island, close to where the vegetation gave way to open water.

"I'm going after her," Peter said. "I've got to get her back."

"No, Wait, Peter. Wait." Brian grabbed his arm.

She stepped onto the island, stood looking out toward the water, and then turned toward shore, facing off to their right. She seemed to hesitate then, turning one way and the other before stopping and staring back at the shore.

"What the heck is she doing?" Peter said.

"I don't know. I don't know."

Without warning she stepped off the small island and walked back toward the shore, her steps as sure as if she were on solid ground. The boys ran down the path along the bog, crashing on through the brush. The heat had penetrated even into the shade of the woods and they were sweating hard when they reached the point she had taken aim on from the center of the bog. Ten feet from shore she went through and they gasped as they watched her drop into the water below. It was only waist deep, but now she was stuck, struggling, against the dense mat of interwoven roots.

"Look, Peter. It's like she's holding something under her left arm and for some reason she can't use her right hand. She'll never get through that way."

Peter jumped into the bog, crashing through, his feet sinking quickly into the thick ooze on the bottom. Eastern toe biters, snapping turtles, none of that mattered now as he waded into the thick leatherleaf, using all his strength to tear it aside and expose the water. The thick vegetation, the roots woven through the thick sphagnum moss, seemed to fight back, but that only caused Peter to fight harder, and in the end the plants could not match his determination to save his sister. Within minutes he had cleared a path for her, and then he took her by the right arm, and she howled as if she were in terrible pain. He let go quickly, drawing back. "Maria! It's me. It's Peter! Follow me to shore." He backed toward the edge of the bog, keeping the path he had cleared open as she followed him into the shallow water and onto dry ground.

Suddenly her eyes changed. They seemed to focus again, and the flat, far away look faded. She looked down at her shorts and sneakers. "What happened? How did I get so wet? How...?" She whirled and looked out at the open water. "I went into the bog, didn't I? I actually went into the bog!"

"Mostly you were on top of it," Brian said. "You went

way out to that high place, and then turned around and came back, and you were almost to shore when you went through." He looked carefully at Maria as he thought about the stick she had broken as if it were a toothpick. "It was awesome!"

"He was there," she said. "Little Louie was there. That's where he hid when they came with the dogs. He hid out there on the bog, and then when he was sure they were gone, he came back. But it was different then. There were lots of trees fallen over with their roots pulled out of the ground, sticking up into the air like giant fans. He was badly hurt. Each step made him bleed more. He couldn't use his right arm. It just hung at his side. He was dying." She whirled around and looked out at the bog. "My god...I could have drowned."

"But you didn't," Brian said.

"I don't think you could have drowned," Peter said. "You did just what Little Louie did. And what that means, Maria, is that Little Louie got back to shore."

"You held your left arm, like you were carrying something. I'll bet he still had the money," Brian said.

"I really did that?"

"What?" Peter asked.

"I really held my arm that way."

Peter nodded. "Bri saw it. And you couldn't use your right arm. Even more weird was that when I tried to pull you out of the bog, you screamed when I touched your arm."

"It was pretty weird, Maria," Brian said.

"Awesome," Peter added. "Absolutely awesome."

Maria cupped her left hand, placed it over her right shoulder and, rotated her arm as if the joint were sore and stiff. "He was really hurting. I think he had been shot in the right arm and shoulder and in the chest. It was hard to breath. It was like sometimes I couldn't seem to get any air, and then all of a sudden it would come with a rush."

"Probably in the lung," Peter said.

"That's why the blood was so bright." Brian looked up, his eyes wide as a terrifying thought tumbled into understanding. "I think it was lucky you came out of it when you did," he said. "I think you could have died just like Little Louie."

"No, it's okay," Maria said. "It's okay." She looked back out across the bog. "Wouldn't you die awfully fast if you were shot that way?"

Her brothers shrugged.

"I mean, in the movies they get right up no matter how badly they're shot, but I don't think that happens in real life. I think someone that badly hurt couldn't have lived very long."

"But he lived long enough to wait until the searchers left," Peter said. "The question is where he went from here." He turned and looked down the deer trail along the edge of the bog. To the right the embankment rose sharply upward, and climbing it would be hard even for someone who hadn't been shot. "Which way, Maria? Which way did he go?"

She pointed to the right. "That way."

In single file with Peter in the lead and Maria last, they followed the trail. The deer had worn it smooth and it was easy walking. Here and there the trail turned and twisted , but it always stayed close to the bog edge and did not climb the steep, heavily forested bank to the right.

Then slowly the bank began to slope downward, folding into the forest floor, offering only a shallow grade, and there the trail forked, one path leading sharply to the right into the

woods, the other still tracking the sinuous edge of the bog.
Peter looked around at Maria. "Now which way?"

"Let's stay close to the bog," Brian said.

"Why?" Peter asked.

"Because it's harder walking in the woods. You have to
duck under the branches and there's stuff to trip over."

Maria stood silently, listening intently, but she could hear
only a soft breeze in the pines and the churning call of an
oven bird far off in the woods. "Bri's right," she said.

As they approached the north shore of the bog the trail
cut off into the woods, and for a way they followed it along
past enormous lichen covered boulders left by the glacier.
They explored around each one, thinking it might hide a cave
or a shelter of some kind that Little Louie could have crawled
into, but they found nothing. Still they kept on, stopping only
when they came to an old cart path. It was overgrown with
small hemlocks and alders, but you could still see the tracks
the wagons had worn into the ground over the years.

"Where do you think it goes?" Maria asked.

They stood in the left hand rut of the old track, but they
could not see far enough in either direction to be sure where
the road might lead. "I can't tell," Peter said

Brian looked up at the sun. "If we go right, we'll come
out in the field. But we should be able to tell, because we'll
have to cross the little stream that comes out of the bog."

"Okay," Maria said. "Let's go." Fear had given way to
the excitement of exploration and the adrenaline rush that
came from exploring a dense unknown woods. She wondered
why she wasn't afraid, especially because she had been afraid
of the woods since the first time she had seen Snow White.

Just before they reached the stream, Peter saw a bottle lying in the leaves to his left, and when he picked it up he saw another. "Wow, look at these. Just like the bottles in Mom's collection." He held one up and handed it to Maria.

"I think these may be even older," Maria said.

Peter and Brian began pulling back the leaves. "Cool," Brian said. "It's an old dump."

"Don't cut yourself," Maria said, but her warning came too late.

"Ouch!" Brian stood up, his left hand clasped onto his right, his eyes squinted against the pain.

"Is it bad?" Maria asked.

"I didn't look. It just hurts."

"Let me see it, Bri." She took his right hand in hers and looked at the long slice along the edge of his hand below his little finger. It didn't look very deep, but it was bleeding steadily. "It's a pretty big cut," she said. "I think you may need to have some stitches."

That got Peter's attention, and he walked over to look at the wound "It's not deep enough to need stitches," he said. "You only need stitches when you have a really deep cut."

"How do you know?" Brian asked. "What do you know about cuts, Peter? I want to go home."

"Remember when I had that cut on my leg. We just taped it together until it scabbed over."

"Nevermind, Peter. We need to get him home. It's still bleeding pretty hard."

Brian pointed to the thick ferns along the road. "Pick some ferns and lay the leaves over the cut. It'll stop the bleeding."

"I don't know whether that's a good idea," Maria said.

"That's what the Indians did," Brian said.

Peter loaded several bottles into his pockets, gave Maria two to carry, and shoved two into Brian's pockets.

"Is that all you can think about?" Maria asked.

"Jeez, Maria, put it to sleep, will you? It's just a cut. It's not even a really bad cut." He clapped his younger brother on the shoulder. "Look, good old Bri isn't even crying." He turned away and headed down the old track to the brook, calling back over his shoulder. "Com'on."

They hopped the rocks over the little brook and then walked up the shallow rising bank through a stand of gray, smooth barked beeches. The beeches gave way to white pine, and suddenly, up ahead, they could see the field. It looked warm and green and very friendly in the sun, and they all liked knowing that home was just on the other side.

"I think the bleeding's nearly stopped," Brian said.

Maria looked at his hand, not the least bit bothered by the blood. "I'm glad I didn't put any ferns on it," she said. "Who knows what kind of bugs live in ferns." She stopped and looked back into the woods. "Whatever you do," she said, "don't say anything about what happened at the bog."

"We gotta get the metal detector and shovel or Dad'll kill us," Brian said.

"He'll probably kill us anyway," Peter said. "I'm pretty sure I forgot to turn the switch off."

"That was cool," Maria said. "He goes absolutely spaz about dead batteries. God, Peter, how could you forget that. We'll hear about it for the rest of the summer." Suddenly Maria noticed the mud on Peter's sneakers and then his wet shorts. "Peter? How did you get so wet?"

"He went into the bog after you," Brian said. "It was neat. Godzilla meets the root monster! You should have seen him ripping and tearing stuff out of his way, and he was growling like a big angry dog."

Maria stopped and looked at her younger brother in disbelief. "You really did that? You came out to save me, even knowing how dangerous it was?"

"I was afraid you might step into a deep spot," he said.

"Peter, I never knew you cared that much about me."

"Jeez, Maria," he said. "I only got one sister."

"Probably one too many," Brian mumbled.

"Oh, thanks, Bri. Here I am taking care of your cut and you start ranking on me."

"Never mind that," Peter said. "How do we explain how we got wet?"

"I'll say that we were rushing to get back because of Brian's cut, and when we went to cross the brook, I fell and Peter jumped in and helped me up."

"Sounds cool,"Peter said.

"Bri?" Maria asked.

"Cool. And I'm sorry about what I said."

Maria smiled. "It's okay, Bri, I know you didn't mean it anymore than I mean some of the nasty things I say to you. It's just part of being brother and sister, I guess." She reached out and fluffed his hair. "And I forgot to thank you for not taking your collecting stuff to the beach."

"Will you guys hurry up," Peter said. "I wanna go for a swim in the pond and get dried off."

Chapter Ten

Whose Money?

"Mom!" Maria rushed into the kitchen. "Brian's got a cut on his hand!"

"I can't hear you," Sarah called from the living room.

"Just come out here!" Maria shouted.

While they waited, Maria led Brian over to the sink and began running the water. "The first thing we have to do is wash it," she said.

Brian pulled his hand away, scowling at his sister. "I think we oughta wait for Mom."

"You have to get the dirt out, Bri. With any cut, the first thing you do is wash it." Her tone was decidedly motherly. "And remember, the glass was in a dump and there's all kinds of bad germs in places like that."

He looked at the water and he knew it was going to hurt, but he also knew that his mother was going to do the same thing so it was only a matter of deciding whether he wanted his sister or his mother to take care of him. He was glad he didn't have to choose.

"What's going on?" Sarah asked as she walked into the kitchen.

"Brian cut his hand on a piece of glass," Peter said. "Doesn't look too bad."

"You'd think it was bad if it was your hand," Brian shot back.

"Com'on, Bri," Peter said as he drifted toward the doorway to the dining room. "It isn't even bleeding anymore. You'll be okay." He looked over at Maria, rolled his eyes toward the second floor, and then slipped out of the room and went upstairs to change into dry clothes.

"Let me see it," Sarah said as she took Brian's hand and held it over the sink, examining the wound in the light from the double windows. "That's quite a cut, Brian. Does it hurt?"

"Naw."

She looked carefully into his eyes. She could see it hurt, but she could also see he was determined not to cry.

"You don't have to be a tough guy," she said. "It's okay to say it hurts."

"It hurts...but just a little."

"It's kind of a long cut, Bri. I'll to have to wash it out to tell how deep it is, and the soap and water will make it sting."

"Soap! You have to use soap? Why do you have to use soap? That'll make it really hurt. Isn't there something else you could use besides soap?" He looked up at his mother and smiled. "Say, I've got an idea," he said using his brightest, most positive tone. "Why don't we just let it alone. Give it a couple of hours to dry up, and then it'll start to heal. Hey, why didn't I think of this before. Sure, that's the way to do it, let it heal up all on its own!"

"It has to be cleaned."

She turned on the water and when it was warm, lathered her hands with soap and then very gently began washing Brian's hand. While she was busy, Maria stepped quietly into the dining room and headed upstairs to change, meeting Peter on the way back down.

"That was easy enough," she said.

"Just don't take too long."

"Okay."

Peter returned to the kitchen, sitting at the table.

"It hurts now," Brian said.

"I'll be quick as I can," Sarah said.

The warm water dissolved the clotted blood, and the cut began to bleed again but now only in a tiny trickle. Sarah held Brian's hand toward the light and examined the wound carefully, pulling it apart at the edges so she could see down into the cut. "You're very lucky," she said. "It's only deep in one place and even that's not very deep. Looks like some ointment and bandages will be all you'll need. No flying trip to the hospital this time."

"Can I go swimming?"

"I think so. But you'll have to put new bandages on afterward." She turned to Peter. "Would you get me the first aid kit from the bathroom cabinet, please, Peter?" There was something else going on here, but she decided to let it go until after she'd finished bandaging the wound. All three of them looked decidedly guilty.

He got the kit and set it on the counter next to the sink

and then stood next to Brian. "Man," he said, "that is a long cut. That's the longest cut I ever saw. Too bad it isn't deeper. You'd have set the family record for stitches." He looked around at his brother. "You're pretty tough, Bri. Me? I would've cried "

Sarah took out the bottle of hydrogen peroxide. "This will sting a little," she said, "but we've got to make sure it's clean."

"That's not gonna sting a little," Brian said, pulling his hand away as he looked at the brown plastic bottle, "that stuff stings a lot!"

Maria walked into the kitchen and over to the counter, standing next to the sink to watch.

"Okay, it stings a lot," Sarah said, "but we still have to make sure the cut is clean."

Brian ground his teeth tightly together, the muscles bunching in hard knots at the corners of his jaw. And it did sting! It stung and it kept on stinging even when Sarah began blowing on it. It stung even worse than when he'd gotten stung by those yellow jackets!

Sarah dried his hand, pulled the bandage box from the kit, took out the ointment and began dressing the wound. "Let me know if it hurts," she said.

"What's going on?" Tom asked as he opened the screen door and walked into the kitchen.

"Just patching up old Bri," Sarah said.

Tom walked over to the sink. "Hey, that's a pretty big cut there, buster. What the heck were you doing? You get attacked by a bear or something?"

"We found an old dump full of bottles in the woods," Peter said, "and we were pulling out the bottles and..." he held up the two he had carried home in his pockets... "Bri was reaching for one and he didn't see a broken one."

"Whoa," Tom said as he picked up one of the bottles and turned it over and over. "You guys have made a real find. "Look at this, Sarah. Am I right here? This looks like the glass that came out of Westford."

"In a minute. I still have two Band Aids to go. Brian, hold still, please."

"I am," he said. But he wasn't, because nobody could hold still when you were getting a cut patched up, especially a big cut like this.

"Where did you find these?" Tom sat down at the kitchen table, picking up each bottle and examining it carefully for the seams which would show that it had been made in a mold instead of having been hand blown.

Maria took two bottles from her pockets and set them on the table. "Brian's got two more."

Tom looked carefully at each bottle. "These are all hand blown."

Sarah finished bandaging Brian's hand. "Now let's see those bottles." She sat down and picked one up, holding it to the light. "Oh, these are great! The last antique show I went to, bottles like these brought forty and fifty dollars apiece, only these are in better shape and..." she turned the bottle over and pointed to a mark in the bottom. "You see this? Dad's right. These were made in Westford and that makes them worth a whole lot more."

"How much?" Brian asked.

"I can't be sure," Sarah said, "but I think maybe three or four hundred dollars each."

"Whoa," Brian said. "We better get back there quick before somebody else finds them."

"You mean people will actually buy these? Somebody would pay that much for an old bottle?" Peter asked.

"You bet they will," Sarah said. "Are there any more?"

"Tons." Maria said. She turned and looked out the windows at the field. She was not thinking about looking for bottles. Another thought had crept in and she wasn't sure where it would lead, but she needed some information. "Dad, what do you think the woods looked like years ago? I mean, would they look any different than they do now?"

"Interesting question. I'm not sure I ever thought about that, but now that you mention it, well, I don't think they change much at all from year to year. A storm might bring down a tree or some branches, but the only big changes occur when someone cuts the timber off or there's a fire. I guess it depends on what you mean by change. There are lots of little changes, but overall, things would look pretty much the same. No, that's not exactly right. Over a long period of time, if the trees hadn't been cut, there would be a big change as the forest approached climax growth. Then the understory disappears and all the trees are big around and very tall, and they shed any branches close to the ground."

She had tried to avoid being specific and raising a lot of questions she didn't want to answer, but it was clear that without being specific she wasn't going to get the information she wanted. "How long would that take?"

"Oh, hundreds of years I think. That's what the forest looked like when the colonists arrived. From what I've read you could walk anywhere in the forest without ever having to bend over."

She didn't want to but she had to narrow it down more. "I was thinking about what the woods might have looked like when..." she glanced at her mother, "I mean around 1940 or so."

Tom grinned and let it pass. "From then till now? Hummm.

I think it would work like this, Maria. If you had set up a time lapse camera, the number of changes would be astonishing, but probably most of them you wouldn't notice from year-to-year because they're so small...no, wait, I'm wrong about that. That was two years after the thirty-eight hurricane. There were trees down everywhere. Big trees, blown right over so the roots stood up on end. I remember seeing a film about it. The damage was unbelievable. The only thing I don't know for sure is how hard it hit this part of the state, but I'd guess, based on what happened in Rhode Island, that it was at least as bad here. A huge number of trees were blown over because the ground was soft and wet from an earlier rain, and when the high winds hit, the roots pulled right out of the ground." He shook his head. "I can get a copy of the tape if you'd like to see what it really looked like."

"Would any of that still show?" Maria glanced around at Peter and Brian, who were busy feigning interest in the bottles.

"I don't know," Tom said. "It's been a long time." He grinned. "Darn interesting question, though. Next time I go into the woods I'll look around."

"When's lunch?" Peter asked.

Sarah stood up and walked over to the refrigerator. "The egg salad's all made, I'll just get the bread, the lettuce, and the milk and you can have at it."

Brian looked down at the bandages on his hand. "Do I have to make my own sandwich? He held up his hand, his lower lip protruded into a pout. "I got a pretty bad injury here, you know."

"I'll make it for you," Maria said.

"First wash your hands," Sarah said.

Peter finished washing first. "Dad, didn't Mr. Barbour say that Little Louie drowned in the bog?"

"I thought so," Tom said.

"We don't think he did," Peter said. Maria and Brian looked at him as if they thought he'd lost his mind.

"What gave you that idea?" Tom asked.

"We took a look at the bog and we think he went out onto it, waited till they gave up searching, and then he came back to shore and hid the money, thinking maybe he could get help somewhere and then come back for it."

"I don't know, Peter," Tom said. "He must have been pretty badly wounded. I don't know how long he could have lasted. Didn't we guess he'd been shot in the lung? I don't know about humans, but I can tell you that any other animal shot through the lungs doesn't last very long."

"Why would he have gone out onto the bog at all?" Sarah asked, allowing her curiosity to draw her into the conversation. "Wouldn't he have known how dangerous it was?"

Tom shook his head. "Might not have," he said. "This is the only bog in this part of the state, and unless you grew up near one or read about them, they don't look dangerous. Someone who grew up in the country might see it, but Little Louie grew up in Providence, as I recall."

Brian looked around at his mother, incredulously. "Jeez, Mom. He had to get away and he must have guessed they'd bring in dogs so he went to the water so the dogs couldn't track him. But he probably knew he had to get far from the shore or the dogs would pick up his scent in the air. My guess is he waded out as far as he could and then climbed up onto the leatherleaf and moss and went way, way out "

"But he'd have left his scent on the leatherleaf," Tom said.

"Not if he did it the way Bri said. Not if he went into the water first, waded out, and then climbed up onto the mat," Peter said.

"That certainly makes sense," Tom said, "but why do you think he didn't go through into the bog?"

"He was called Little Louie," Brian said. "Remember, Mr. Barbour said how he sat really low in the seat of the car? He was probably so light that he didn't fall through."

Tom nodded. "It's a pretty good theory," he said, "and if I follow it, what you're saying is that if he got out onto the bog without falling through, he could have made it back to shore."

"Right," Peter said. "He wouldn't have stayed there."

"But with his wound," Tom said, "he could have stayed so long stiffened up and couldn't get back. That's what happens to a deer." He grinned. "I do see where this is leading," he said. "If he got back to shore then he must have buried the money and then tried to get away."

"That's the way I see it," Brian said.

"What I'd like to know," Maria said, "is who the money belongs to."

"An interesting point," Tom said. "From what I've read the money came from illegal gambling. I think that makes it a case of finder's keepers. I don't know what the IRS would say about that, but I guess if I found it, I wouldn't tell a soul."

Sarah was stunned. "Tom, how can you say that? That's against the law."

Tom sort of grunted. "You know how I feel about the IRS. They're nothing more than a way to take money from the people who earn it and give it to those who don't care to work. It's all social politics. Just another way to get votes."

It was not a subject Sarah liked to discuss and she particularly did not want to discuss it in front of the kids. Once they had agreed in matters of politics, but over time Tom had grown more and more conservative, and while she had to agree with some of his points, she did not agree with breaking the law. "It simply isn't honest," she said.

"Maybe it is and maybe it isn't," Tom said. "But it's got to where the government thinks they have a right to the money we earn, and that's nothing short of stealing. Worse, they take that money and spend it on bureaucrats who end up telling us what to do. And look at what'll happen when my folks die. All they've got is the farm, but there's so much land that by the time the government gets through figuring out the inheritance taxes, Jack and I will have to sell the farm to cover the taxes. That land has been in the family for over two hundred years and we want to keep it that way, but you can bet the government won't allow that. They'll force us to sell because of the inheritance taxes, and worse, they'll base those taxes on the value of the farm today without considering what the value of the dollar was when the farm was bought. Which means the taxes will be based on inflation, and the main cause of inflation is the government because they print the money, and the more they print the less each dollar is worth."

Peter grinned. "Hold the lecture, Dad." It was the code they'd developed years ago to warn their father that he was going on too long.

He grinned back. "Did it again, huh?"

"What's the IRS?" Maria asked.

"The Internal Revenue Service," Tom said. "The people who collect the taxes on the money we earn."

"The government takes away our money?" Peter looked genuinely surprised.

"God, Peter," Maria said. "What planet have you been living on? I Mean, like, there isn't anyone who doesn't know what taxes are."

"I just never thought about who paid them before. How much do we pay?"

"Thirty-three percent of what I earn just to the federal government. Forty-six percent overall." Tom shook his head. "Maybe I wouldn't be so angry, if the government would mind its own business, but that's not the way it works. They just go on spending more and more and more on all sorts of dumb programs that only keep government workers employed."

"How much is forty-six percent?" Maria asked.

"Jeez, Maria." Peter shook his head slowly. Now it was his turn. "It's almost half."

Tom took a carrot from the vegetable plate, broke it into two pieces and then set them on the table, the pieces lying end-to-end. "The whole carrot represents what I make in a year." He picked up one piece and popped it into his mouth. "That's what's left after taxes."

"Maybe you better switch to celery," Brian said. "At least it tastes better than those soapy old, crummy old carrots. I don't understand why we have to eat stuff like that anyway. What's the use of having to suffer when you eat?"

They all laughed and Brian looked quite pleased with the success of his joke.

"Just don't go to broccoli," Peter said and they all began laughing harder, because getting Peter to eat even a single broccoli branch was like trying to crack a cement wall with your head.

As the laughter died down, Tom set his sandwich on the plate. "And even if Little Louie did make it back to shore, who's to say he had the money with him? He could have ditched it anywhere between here and Hartford."

"Dubious, Dad," Maria said.

"Why? He could have tossed it out of the car."

"The other car was too close," Peter said.

"Oh, the money's there all right," Brian said. "Lying as it

has for fifty-seven years, somewhere between the bog and
the high dry ground where the white oaks grow — somewhere there, somewhere near where the raven roosts in a sil-
very red oak snag."

Dead silence.

Then, finally, Sarah spoke. "Brian, that was pure poetry.
That was wonderful!"

"Where do you come up with that stuff, Bri?" Tom said.
"No, wait, I know where, and I'll bet anything you guys don't
know this. Your mother was once a very promising poet. She
won all the prizes when we were in college, she had her work
published in the journals, and she almost got a book of po-
ems published."

"Mom?" Maria looked as if she'd just been told that the
cutest boy in school was in love with her. "You were a poet?
And you won prizes? I can't believe it! I mean I can believe
it, but it's still a surprise. That is just so neat! Why didn't you
ever tell us?"

"It was a long time ago."

"Why did you stop?" Maria asked.

"I don't know. We got married and I went to work and
then you guys started coming along, and after that I just kind
of forgot about my poetry."

"Maybe it's time to start again," Tom said. "These guys
can pretty much take care of themselves now."

Maria's enthusiasm was balanced by Peter's skepticism.
Had he inherited that too? How could you be a ballplayer and
write poetry? No way. Anybody who could write poetry,
couldn't be an athlete. Just look at Bri. He could do almost
anything except catch a baseball or a football. On the other
hand he could ice skate like a madman. No one in the family
could skate like Bri. Could a hockey player write poetry? But

suppose he turned out to be one of those figure skaters? There was something a little iffy about some of those guys. Naw. Not Bri. He liked knocking people down too much. Every chance he got on the playground he took somebody out, and he was always getting into trouble with his teachers because he was too rough. Straight A's in all his subjects and D's in behavior. But maybe, and it was a definite maybe, if a kid as tough as Bri could write poetry there was nothing wrong with it. One thing he knew, though, was that he couldn't have put the words together the way Bri had.

"Could you show us your poetry?" Maria asked.

"I'd have to find it first and I have no idea where it is after this move."

"I know where it is," Brian said as he bit into the second half of his sandwich. "It's in a box near the top of the attic stairway. Can't miss it. Says, 'Sarah's Poetry,' right there on the top."

Everyone looked around at him and then smiled.

"Jeez, Bri," Peter said, "did you memorize every box?"

Brian grinned. "I tripped over it. Nearly fell down the attic stairs."

"What's for dessert?" Peter asked.

"My special peanut butter cookies."

"All right!"

"But not until all the vegetables disappear. And I don't mean some measly little tidbits either, I mean a handful."

"I only eat red vegetables," Brian said looking at the celery, carrots, and broccoli as if they might form into a battle line and attack him from across the table.

"I've got some nice fresh radishes...." Sarah said.

Brian's face squeezed into a grimace. "Guess I'll try the celery." He picked a short stalk from the plate on the lazy

Susan in the center of the table, then held it up, turning it over several times as if it were most certainly poisonous. "Why do they make all this stuff green and yellow? How come it isn't white like mashed potatoes?" He shook his head. "Do I have to eat the whole thing?"

"Yes, you do," Sarah said.

"But, Mom, it's green! And look at the size of it. There's enough in one stalk to choke an elephant. How about we cut us a deal here. Suppose I eat just half of it now and then have the other half at supper."

"No celery, no...."

"I know...no cookies." He picked the smallest stalk of celery he could find, inspected it, then reached for the salt and holding the stalk over his plate, covered every inch, making sure to load up the concave stem.

"Brian! Stop that! A little salt is okay, but you put enough on that celery to melt the ice off the driveway," Sarah said.

"But, Mom, it tastes really terrible without salt."

"Too much salt isn't good for you."

"I didn't take all that much, and anyway, I need salt because I'll be sweating. I read that in a book. When it's hot and you sweat you need to eat a lot of salt to replace what you lose when you sweat."

Short of washing off the stalk of celery and making him start over, Sarah could think of no way to end the dispute. Even that wouldn't have ended it. He'd surely have thrown a fit and wound up in his room. It wasn't worth it.

Peter grabbed a carrot and Maria took a medium sized broccoli tree.

"How can you eat that?" Peter asked.

"It's good," Maria said, refusing to be drawn into another squabble.

"Ugh. I'd rather eat dog...."

"Enough!" Sarah said, cutting Peter off before he could finish. "I don't want to hear anymore about this. Just eat the vegetables."

Slowly the required number of vegetables disappeared, the cookies arrived, and the mood improved rapidly.

"Brian," Tom said, "didn't you tell me you saw a raven out at the end of the field?"

"Yup. We all did."

"I'd like to get a look at him. Maybe we could take a walk out to that dump you guys found and do a little treasure hunting. Those bottles are a real find."

"Do you think it's safe?" Sarah asked.

"Oh, sure. We'll all wear work gloves and I've got a couple of old clam hooks that are ideal for raking through a dump." He slid his chair back from the table. "Com'on, who knows what we'll find."

As they walked into the barn to get the clam hooks, Peter let his hand trail down the side of the purple car, his index finger tracing the shiny chrome strip that ran the length of the car. "Did you get it running yet?" he asked.

"Not yet, Peter, and it's a pretty good mystery. I've changed every single part I can think of and all it does is crank and crank and now it never even coughs." He shook his head. "I think I'm going backward. But I'll get it going if I have to replace every nut and bolt in the engine. I never saw a motor I couldn't get to run, and I worked on some pretty rough old engines when I was in high school."

"I'd like to help," Peter said.

"Sure. That'd be great."

"I think it's time I learned about cars and how they work. After all, I'll be driving pretty soon."

His father grinned. "Pretty handy stuff to know. And if you get good enough at it, you can get yourself a junker and fix it up, and then by the time you get your license you'll have a car to drive. We can even make a road around the field, and you can practice on that."

"Whoa, way cool."

"It's a lot of work, but it's also a lot of fun."

"I'll need to earn some money," Peter said.

"I think I can find jobs for you guys to do around here."

"Where I would find a junker?"

"Lots of places. Walter Barbour's got two old pickups out back of his barn, and I'll bet he'd part with one of 'em."

"When can we ask him?"

Tom grinned. "First help me get Little Louie's car running, and then you'll know whether you really want to put in that much work."

At the back of the barn they picked up the two hooks and three burlap sacks and then walked out to where Brian and Maria waited by the door.

"I'd sure like to see that raven," Tom said as they headed out toward the field. "Darn unusual to see one so far south."

Chapter Eleven

Little Louie's Spirit?

They sat in the sun on the long stone back step washing the bottles they had dug from the dump. To make the work go faster they had divided the job, Brian placing the bottles into a large tub of soapy water, Peter washing the outsides of the bottles, and Maria scrubbing the insides with a bottle brush. They took turns rinsing the bottles with the hose.

"I hope we get some of the money from these when Mom sells them," Peter said. "Especially after all this work."

"It's a lot of bottles," Brian said, thinking about how many more there were in the dump.

"Is that all you guys ever think about? Money? Do you have to get paid for everything you do?"

"They're our bottles," Peter said. "We found them."

"But on land which belongs to Mom and Dad."

"Actually, it wasn't," Brian said. "The dump is just on the other side of the property line."

"Then we stole 'em ," Maria said.

"Finders keepers," Brian said.

"A dump, Maria, is a place where people throw things they don't want."

She nodded. "I just think we ought to do the job and not think about getting a share of the money. Look at all the things we get. Isn't that enough?"

Peter looked back down at the bottle he held in his hand. He hated it when an argument went this way because he had no answer. Sure they got a lot of things, but somehow this was different, and he couldn't quite explain why. Nevermind. Maria was just wrong. They found the bottles, they were doing the work, the money was theirs. But their parents would sell them, and that was something you got paid for. The way he saw it, equal shares would be the way to go.

He pulled another bottle from the water, looking around at the two full sacks. On some of them the dirt came away easily, while on others the dirt was so stubborn it seemed to have become part of the glass, and no amount of scrubbing worked. They'd just have to soak for awhile.

"Tell me again," Maria said. "What exactly did I do?"

Peter looked around to make sure their parents were not within earshot. "You went into a kind of a trance. I mean, it was really weird. You couldn't hear anything we said, and when I tried to stop you, you knocked me off the path into the bushes. It was awesome, Maria, really and truly awesome.

You brushed me out of the way as if I weighed nothing at all, and then Brian shoved a big stick between your legs, and you broke it like was a twig."

"But why isn't there a mark on my legs? Shouldn't there have been a mark?" She stretched out her legs, but even in the bright sun they could see no marks on her legs.

It was a real thick branch," Brian said.

"What did I do then?"

"You just walked right out onto the bog. I thought you were going to go through, but you walked out to a kind of an island, and then you turned and walked back to shore.

"And then you said he was still alive," Brian added.

She sat quietly, hugging her legs, looking down toward the pond. "If I tell you something, promise you won't think I'm crazy."

"Sure," Peter said.

"Is it scary?" Brian asked.

"Kinda."

He sighed. "I don't like being scared."

"Even so, I think I have to tell you."

"Well...if you have to...."

"I could hear his voice as clearly as I can hear yours now. It was very raspy and harsh, and it scared me. It was very, very nasty."

"Now I'm scared," Brian said.

"But I wasn't scared," Maria said, "that's what's so weird. I wasn't scared then, and I'm not scared now. How do you explain that? And how come the sight of the blood spooked me but hearing his voice didn't?"

"You must've heard his spirit," Brian said. "And besides,

when you heard his voice you were still in a trance, and nothing could have scared you then."

"But why did she say he's still alive?" Peter asked. "Spirits are what's left after someone's dead."

Maria stood up suddenly. "Wait, I understand. I understand what it means! When we first saw the blood on the seat it was fifty-seven years to the day he was shot. Then we saw the blood on the trail and then came the bog...it's perfectly clear. Don't you see what's happening?"

"Things are happening the same way they did fifty-seven years ago," Brian said.

"Exactly!"

Peter looked at them as if they had both gone south. "Do you actually believe that?"

"I don't know what I believe," Maria said, "but it's just like Brian said. People who were murdered and didn't get a proper burial sometimes come back to haunt the place where they were killed. Only when the remains are found and buried does the ghost go away."

"That's all made up stuff," Peter said.

"No it isn't, Peter. You can read about it in a book in our own library. And anyway, if it's made up, how do you explain the blood?" Maria asked. "And how do you explain what happened to me."

Peter shrugged.

"I'm not even sure I can go back out there," Maria said. "It's not that I'm afraid, it's just that I don't want him to take over my mind again. What if he never gave it back? I'd end up like a zombie. The walking dead."

"But we have to," Peter said, "because we have to find

the money. I know it's there, I just know it. I can feel it. After he came out of the bog, Little Louie buried the money."

"Pretty good chance the mice ate it," Brian said.

"Or Dad's right, and he ditched it before he got here," Maria added.

"Or there was never any money," Brian said

Peter looked over at them, astonished. "What happened to you guys? I thought you believed the money was there."

"I don't know," Brian said.

"Me either," Maria said.

"I think you're both spooked."

"Okay, if that's what you want to believe," Maria said.

"That's not the point," Peter shot back. "The point is that the money is there. All we have to do is figure out where."

Maria sat down on the warm stone step, drawing her legs up and once again wrapping her arms around her knees. "I thought it was really weird that when we went out there with Dad, the raven wasn't there." She looked around at Peter, shading her eyes from the sun. "And he wasn't there the last time either."

"So?" Peter looked around at her.

"I think the raven is his spirit," Maria said.

"Holy shit!" Peter said.

"And when we don't see it, that's the most dangerous time because that's when it can take over your mind," Maria said.

"If I wasn't scared before, that did it," Brian said. "I just wish there wasn't any chance the money was there because then I wouldn't have to worry about whether I was going out there ever again."

They heard the phone ring and Maria looked around

quickly and then back down at the tub full of bottles. She didn't have to wonder when the phone rang now. It was never for her. Then a minute or two later Sarah stepped out onto the porch. "Maria, it's for you."

"What?"

"The phone."

"I've got a phone call?" She jumped up and ran into the house. Who could it be? Was it one of her friends? It had to be. Who else did she know?

Brian looked into the tub and stirred the bottles. "We won't find anything just sitting here," he said. "We have to be brave enough to go out there and explore, and Maria has to go with us. Nothing will happen unless she's there."

Peter shook his head. "That stuff about spirits is pretty hard to take, Bri. It's like the stuff in a horror story or some really nasty movie, and none of that stuff is true. It's just made up, you know, like fiction."

"But you saw it happen," he said.

"I know, but I'm just not sure if I believe what I saw."

"Jeez, Peter, how can you not believe what you saw?"

"I don't know." He looked into the tub full of bottles. "All I know is that what I saw scared me worse than any movie I ever saw. I also know I still have to go back out there no matter how much I don't want to, because I know the money's there, and I figure you maybe get one chance like this in a lifetime, and there's no way I'm gonna miss it."

"Then let's go," Brian said.

"We can't go because we gotta do these bottles." Peter hoped Brian wouldn't see through his excuse.

"They'll keep."

"We still have to wait for Maria," Peter said.

"Then let's clean a few bottles while we wait. She could be on the phone for hours." Brian pulled a medium sized bottle from the tub and scrubbed the outside of it while Peter worked the bottle brush around the inside of another bottle. The dirt came free easily now, and when each had finished, they switched bottles.

They had washed nearly half the bottles by the time Maria came back out and sat down on the steps. "That was Mariel."

"What'd she want?" Peter asked.

"She invited Brian and me over for the afternoon."

"Cool," Brian said. He was always ready to go.

Peter pulled another bottle from the tub and began running the brush in and out. "Are you gonna go?" He asked.

"Mom said it was okay." Maria sat down. "Peter, maybe you could call Mariel's other brother and invite him over."

"Naw. I'm gonna sort baseball cards. I'm way behind." There was no point in calling. If he wanted to see him he'd have asked him over too. "And I still haven't unpacked all the boxes from moving. Maybe I can get that done and then Mom will get off my case about it."

"I'm sorry," Maria said. "It doesn't seem very fair. I thought you two were getting along fine at the beach."

"It's okay," Peter said, but she was right. It just wasn't fair, and it pissed him off that he didn't have anywhere to go. On the other hand, for awhile he would have the whole place to himself, and that wasn't a luxury he got very often. "Hey," he said, "it's okay. He's probably got soccer practice or something. Maybe I oughta find out about that. Maybe they've got a league I could play in."

"Ask Mom to check into it for you," Maria said. "But promise me one thing, Peter, okay? Promise me you won't go out there alone?"

"I might look for a place to build a good tree house after I finish my cards. I've got a lot of cards that need to be sorted." He smiled up at his sister. It was hard to feel jealous of her for having been invited to Mariel's when she was being so nice. But it was also hard to be nice when you felt as left out of things as he felt just now. "If I wanted, I could invite him over, but it'll be nice just to have some time to myself. And anyway, it'll give me a chance to think about all this stuff."

"What's to think about?" Brian asked. "It's perfectly clear that the spirit talks to Maria, and that's how we'll find the money."

Maria shook her head, then looked toward the kitchen as they heard Sarah drop the car keys into her purse. "What worries me is what he's going to want in exchange."

"Maybe I'll just read some comics for awhile."

"Peter, I'd feel a lot better if you didn't go out there alone," Maria said. "Promise me you won't."

"I'll wait till you get back," he said as he ran his soapy hand back over his head to chase away a deer fly, and left a tall rooster comb of soap suds.

"That's cool," Maria said with her usual sarcasm.

"Really cool." Brian started laughing.

"What the heck are you laughing at?"

"The soap," Brian said as he gasped for air.

Peter still hadn't gotten the joke, and then out of the corner of his eye he spotted his reflection in the sliding doors. "Whoa! Look at that! It's Lizard Man!" He jumped to his feet and began to stalk around like a lizard, letting his tongue slither out from between his teeth, hissing as he talked. "Descended from the giant Komodo dragon lizards, he stalks the world seeking delectable prey...." He looked up as Sarah stepped out onto the stone porch. "Suddenly the lizard freezes, waiting motionless as prey approaches."

"Look out, Mom," Brian shouted, "Peter's turned into Lizard Man!"

"What on earth!"

"Slowly the lizard swivels his head, his catlike eyes fixed on his prey. At any second he will strike...."

"Run for the car!" Sarah laughed, as she quickly joined the game. "I've seen these lizard devils before."

Brian and Maria ran for the car, as Peter scurried after them, bent at the waist, swiveling himself in the middle from side-to-side, hissing, and wiggling his tongue. "Lizard Man watches in dismay as his victims flee to the safety of an impenetrable cage." Brian and Maria quickly wound up the windows. "Undaunted, he attacks!" Peter began clawing at the closed windows. "Sooner or later they must come out for food and water, and in the meantime, Lizard man waits!"

Sarah started the car, checking carefully to make sure she could see Peter, before putting it into gear and backing up into the turnaround.

Peter watched them leave, then ran his hand back over his head and removed the soapsuds. He turned toward the house, feeling a little sad and a little sorry for himself. It was times like this, he thought, when you really needed to have a dog around.

Chapter Twelve

Words of the Raven

For awhile he resorted to reading his Spiderman comics just to get his mind off being left behind. But it was hard not to think about it. After all, he'd been left out, and nobody liked that. He finally set the comic aside and lay on his back with his hands behind his head, staring up at the ceiling. It needed painting. So did the walls. Nothing was going his way. And then he remembered his talk with Dad about getting a junker and making it run, and that helped for awhile, but then his mood drifted back to dark.

The truth was, everything sucked and there was nothing he could do about it. There wasn't even anyone to blame.

Until somebody invited him somewhere, he had no life at all. He rolled onto his side and looked out the window. From the second floor the field looked much smaller than it did when you walked up into it from the pond. There, because of the way the land rolled away from you, the field seemed to go on and on as if the end were always moving away.

And then, suddenly, like a scene shift in a movie, it all changed. The grass was deep and instead of green it was tan, and the trees at the edges of the field were smaller, and here and there, back in the woods, he could see great root fans rising where huge trees had been felled by the wind. He rubbed his eyes, but the vision seemed to intensify. He could hear the sound of crows in the trees, and in the distance the roar of an engine drawing closer and closer, and he turned his head to the left, trying to see past the house and barn, but he could not, and then suddenly a car, the Purple Car, except that it was black and not purple, came flying past the barn and the pond and shot up into the field. It slowed going up the first low hill, and then picked up speed as it raced past the pines. And then another car, a big fancy car with lots of chrome and fat, white-sided tires, roared past the barn and up into the field, following the track through the grass.

The first car stopped and he saw a small man wearing a gray hat and a dark suit climb out carrying a satchel. Little Louie. It was Little Louie LaMontaigne, and even from this distance, Peter could see the long scar across his chin. Just then the second car broke over the rise, and Little Louie jumped back into his car and tried to start it. But he must have flooded it, and Peter could hear the starter grinding and grinding, but the engine just wouldn't catch, and then suddenly it fired and a great black cloud of smoke came out of the exhaust pipe, and then the engine died. The second car stopped, skidding sideways in the tall grass, and two men leaped out, one of them carrying a machine gun. He dropped onto one knee, steadied the barrel on the hood of the car and opened fire. A long rolling burst of gunshots smashed against his ears, and Peter could see the bullets hit the Ford, and he saw Louie jump in his seat and then slump out of sight.

For a time it was quiet. Then the driver of the second car climbed out on the passenger side, and keeping low, using the car as a shield, slipped toward the front of the car where the machine gunner still rested his gun, the smoke rising steadily from the barrel.

"I think I hit him," the machine gunner said.

"Give him a minute," the driver said. "He could be waiting for us to get close."

As if from nowhere, another figure appeared. A tall, broad shouldered man, he walked with long strides up onto the highest point in the field. At the end of his right arm he carried a long, heavy looking rifle. Hec Chandler. It had to be. But what surprised Peter was how deadly he looked. He was a farmer, just a farmer, but by comparison the gunmen looked like innocent kids. And then he put his rifle to his shoulder and fired. The blast of sound seemed impossibly loud as it roared across the field and echoed off the trees and hills.

The bullet hit the machine gunner in the back, picked him up, and threw him onto the hood of the car. The second shot hit the driver in the middle of the chest as he turned toward the sound. The third man tried to run, but Hec was too fast and the bullet hit him in the thigh.

What caught Peter's eye next was a movement in the grass just past the first car. Little Louie was crawling slowly away.

But Hec, standing where he was, could not see him. He did not once even glance that way as Little Louie wedged himself through the grass like a fat, black snake.

"Put your gun up on the car where I can see it and come out with your hands up!" Hec called.

No answer. The air had gone dead still and the only sounds came from the distant calls of birds deep in the woods. He heard another vehicle coming, a pickup, shooting out from behind the barn, and then stopping at the edge of the field.

He wore overalls, a felt hat, and a plain blue shirt, and he too carried a rifle. He pointed toward the pines, and Hec put his rifle to his shoulder and waited. It was Mr. Barbour, young and slender, and he walked quickly through the grass, and then disappeared into the thick green of the trees. For several minutes it was quiet with only the sound of an occasional bird, and then he heard Mr. Barbour shout. "Drop that pistol or I'll drop you dead as the others!"

The gunman had no choice. He tossed his pistol up onto the roof of the car. "I'm bad shot, I can't stand up!"

As they moved in on the car, Little Louie slipped off into the woods. Once or twice Peter saw the dark suit among the trees and then he was gone.

The scene dissolved like a movie, one scene fading into another. The Ford still sat in the field, but the other car was gone, and the hay had been beaten flat over a large area. Hec walked into the field behind two big brown horses. He steered the team around to the back of the car, stopped, and let the reins fall to the ground. He walked to the driver's door, opened it, and climbed in. The engine began to grind and sputter, coughing black smoke, but it didn't start.

Hec climbed out of the car. "Probably got a hex on it now," he muttered. He backed the horses up to the front of the car, hooked onto the bumper, and hauled the brand new car out of the field and up into the woods.

That done, he unhooked the team, steered them across the field, and hooked them to a mowing machine. He started cutting at the outside edge, working in counterclockwise fashion. Peter watched them grow smaller and smaller, the sound of the cutter bar and Hec's voice, calm and steady as he instructed his horses, fading into the distance, the image rippling in the heat waves wriggling over the field.

Just as he reached the end of the field a large black bird seemed to rise up from the ground. Twice it circled out over the field, calling in a harsh raspy voice before landing in a big dead tree. There he ruffled his feathers and preened them, shifting his weight from foot to foot. Then he called again, a harsher sound this time, and louder by far. With each call he bobbed up and down on the branch.

Hec stopped to watch, and the bird dropped from the branch, opened its wings, soared out over the field, and wheeled back into the woods. Hec clucked to his team, dropped the reins on their backs, and returned to mowing.

The vision, as quickly as it had begun, disappeared. Peter shook his head and rubbed his eyes. Had he really seen it or had it been his imagination? Imagination. It had to be. After all, he knew the story because Mr. Barbour had told it to them. But he had not mentioned the raven.

He rolled onto his back and stared up at the ceiling. What

did it mean? Did it mean anything at all or was he just stressing out? He climbed off the bed and as he passed his desk he picked up his small notebook and pencil and stuffed them into the pocket of his shorts. He jogged down the stairs and out into the kitchen. Mom hadn't gotten back yet and Dad was out in the barn working on the car.

He crossed through the heavy heat hovering above the asphalt drive. "Any hope?" he asked as he stepped into the shady barn.

"Gosh darn strange," Tom said. "It just won't run."

Peter looked down into the engine well, but it made no sense to him. "What could be wrong with it?"

"It acts like it's flooded. Tell you what. You climb in and push the starter when I tell you, okay?"

"Sure."

Tom reached in and took the air cleaner off the carburetor. "Okay, push the starter," he said.

Peter pushed his foot down on the starter and the engine began to crank.

"Okay, stop," Tom called. He stood up, scratching his head. "Sure doesn't look like it's getting too much gas."

Peter climbed out of the car. "How come it doesn't do that big smoking thing anymore?"

"It does if you keep cranking. I've checked the timing half-a-dozen times and it's dead on."

Peter thought if he were smart he'd just stay here and learn about car engines, but he had other things to do, though if you had asked him, he could not have told you exactly what those things were. "I'm going for a walk," he said.

"Where?"

"I'm gonna go find a good place to build a tree fort."

"Stay within range, okay?"

"Yup."

Tom pulled himself out from under the hood of the car, wiping his hands. "Maybe we could have a catch later."

"Cool," Peter said.

"Give me a holler when you get back. I'll probably still be working on the car." He laughed. "In fact I know I'll still be working on the car." He shook his head. "I'm gonna hate having to go back to work next week if it isn't running."

◆ ◆ ◆

Peter cut into the woods behind the barn, circled the south end of the pond, and then walked in a straight line back to where the car had sat. Already a few blades of grass had sprung up, and he wondered how long it would take before all signs of the car disappeared. He walked onto the barren patch and scraped here and there with his feet the way you do when you step into the batter's box, or when you're starting to look for something small you have lost.

In truth, he *was* looking for something, though he could not have said what...just...something, and it was something small. The air seemed especially still and close and the mosquitoes closed in quickly. He slapped and swatted to keep them off, but they still got through.

Several times he looked up, listening, straining against the silence, but all he could hear was the heavy thumping of a farm tractor somewhere in the distance. What do I expect to find? He swept his right foot through the dry dirt, scraping away soil with each pass. There's nothing here. This is stupid. I'm just way, way too intense about this.

He slapped a mosquito that had lit on the back of his neck, then looked down at the bloody spot on the palm of his hand. If I don't get out of here these things will eat me alive, he thought, but he did not leave. And then, as he swept aside another patch of dirt, he saw something, and he squatted down and picked it up. A bullet.

He stood up, turning it over and over in his fingers, wondering what to make of it. The end had been badly smashed, and he guessed that must have happened when it came through the metal of the door. But it had some odd, dark stains, unlike the bullets they had found inside the car.

Blood? Were they blood stains? Was this the bullet that had gone through Little Louie? Maybe he hadn't been as badly wounded as they thought. Maybe, once the bleeding stopped, he could have lived for days, and that meant that Maria's story made sense, no matter how weird it had sounded.

The cry of the raven close by brought his head up sharply. The bird sat in a dead tree by the edge of the field, looking down at him, watching him. In a shaft of sunlight that had found its way down through the trees, the bird's feathers shimmered in the sun, showing almost as much purple as they did black. For several minutes he stood, watching the raven, then suddenly he called, "what do you want?"

The raven seemed to wag its head slowly from side-to-side. Then it looked up, opened its black bill, and made a series of gurgles. A few seconds later it repeated the sounds.

But now the odd sounds seemed familiar. Where had he...in the vision...they were the same sounds the bird had made when he had flown up out of the field in front of Hec's horses. "Are you trying to tell me something?" Peter asked. The next thought set a wave of shivers dancing up his spine. Of course it was trying to tell him something. But what?

They hadn't made any sense to Hec Chandler, and though they didn't make a whole lot of sense to him either, he knew enough not to ignore them. He looked up at the great, black bird as it rattled out the sounds again. He dug the note pad from his shorts, pulled the short pencil from beneath the ring binder, and opened to a clear page. "Now, say it again."

The raven obliged. "*Cldndlnlybvdgrnd.*" Peter wrote furiously, fighting to find letters which duplicated what he heard. The raven waited several seconds and then began a different series of sounds. "*Brydbnsnddtrzrbfnd.*" Peter looked down at what he had written. Could it possibly make any sense? It was just a jumble of letters. If he hadn't had phonics in school he couldn't even have written them down.

The raven gurgled in his usual fashion, dropped from the limb of the tree, spread his wings, wheeled, and flew back across the open field, disappearing into the thick dark green of the pines and hemlocks.

Peter snapped his note pad closed, stuck the pencil into the ring binder at the top, and then stuffed them into his pocket as he looked around to see whether anyone had seen him. What kind of a nut bag was he turning into? Writing down bird sounds as if they could possibly mean something? Talk about playing with a short deck. He shook his head, stepped out into the field, and with long determined strides, head down, he walked back to the house. If anybody caught him doing stuff like this, they'd make him into a special ed student. He grinned at that, and then his thoughts drifted ahead as he tried to guess what it would be like at his new school. He thought it might be okay, based on the kids he had met at the beach. He wasn't worried about grades. He hated having homework, but he always did the work.

He came up into the yard, aware that the tractor he had been hearing was their tractor, and as he looked up, here came dad driving the tractor and towing a trailer with an old pick up truck on it.

"Wow!" he shouted as he ran toward the driveway. He'd done it. He'd gone and gotten one Mr. Barbour's old trucks. Mom was gonna blow a gasket, but who cared. This was gonna be phenomenally cool.

Chapter Thirteen

Breaking the Code

His father backed the trailer up to the door of the back shed and waited for Peter to swing open the doors. Then he backed the trailer halfway into the shed. Finally he released the chain and let the trailer tip back, and using the cable from the winch on the power take-off to keep a strain on the truck, he slowly let it roll down onto the concrete floor. The last thing he did was climb back up on the tractor and draw it out from under the truck. There it sat in the middle of the single bay shed and Peter could hardly believe it. A truck, his truck, and all they had to do was get it running.

He walked around the truck, opened the door and, climbed in. It was in pretty ratty shape, he thought, a lot worse than the purple car. He wiped the dust off the speedometer. Wow, only seventy thousand miles.

"Well, whattya think?" Tom asked.

"It's neat, Dad, it's really neat. Will it run?"

"Not yet. Walt says it needs a valve job, rings, brakes, and probably a whole lot of other stuff."

"It's only got seventy thousand miles on it."

"Well, that's more like two hundred and seventy-thousand. It's been around twice."

"How much did you pay for it?"

"Not a dime. Walt was glad to get rid of it." Tom smiled. "Way it works," he said, "is that sometime Walt will need a favor, and now he'll feel free to ask."

"But isn't it an antique?"

"Until it's running it's a junker." He shook his head. "It'll be a lot of work," he said. "We'll have to pull the body off completely and get all the rust off the frame, and then work up from there. In the meantime, we can pull the engine apart and do the valves and the rings and whatever else we find."

"That's okay. If I can learn how to do it, then I'll know how to fix cars, and that's always a good thing to know."

His father grinned, anticipating the fun ahead. "But first I'm going to get Little Louie's car running." He started out of the shed. "Be sure to latch the doors."

"Okay," Peter said. He stuffed his hands into his pockets and his right hand found his note book. There was plenty of time to look at the truck, he thought, and right now he had something else he had to do. He closed the doors, swung the hasp over, dropped the pin in place, and headed for the house. It was gonna take some time to figure out what the raven had said, and he wanted to finish before Maria and Brian got home.

For awhile Peter sat at the kitchen table looking down at

the sheet of white paper, his pencil poised and ready as he stared at the letters he had copied.

cldndlnlybvdgrnd
brydbnsnddtrzrbfnd

Did that make any sense? All he could see was a jumble of letters all run together. He looked out through the wide double windows at the pond. The wind had come up and the surface of the water in the bright sun looked as if someone were shaking a wrinkled piece of aluminum foil. For awhile he stared at the water and the hypnotic patterns.

Then he looked away from the flashing glitter and focused again on the problem. He understood that what he had done was write down sounds, not words. So what he had to do now was put the sounds into words. It was no different than what they did in comic books when they made words like *ouch* or *aiiieeee* or *aaaggghhh*. He looked down at the letters again, staring at them, trying to make them fall into some kind of pattern. Nothing. What he needed was food. Junk food. Once you had something to munch on you could think better.

He prowled the pantry, checking here and there, finally coming up with an opened bag of potato chips. The only question was whether to take the whole bag or just a handful. No problemo. Had to be the bag. He carried it back to the table and began nibbling away, trying to make them last, but finally just stuffing them into his mouth, savoring the salt and the oil, and the way they started out crisp and wound up in a wonderfully salty, oily mash.

Now he needed something to drink, and because of his mother's new rule, there was no soda in the house. What he wouldn't have given for a nice cold Pepsi. If only we hadn't pigged out on the stuff, Mom wouldn't have gone crazy and banned soda. As far as he was concerned, they hadn't pigged out at all, but then the kid's votes didn't count. He found a pitcher of lemonade in the refrigerator, poured a glass, left the pitcher on the counter, and walked back to the table.

Even knowing what he'd written down was no help. The letters still didn't make any sense. Probably it was all just his imagination, which would have been a lot easier to believe if everyone hadn't always said he wasn't the most imaginative kid ever born. Heck, he didn't even get scared in scary movies when everybody else was shaking and screaming.

Maria was the one with the imagination. He was good at stuff like math and science where you had facts and numbers to deal with. Real stuff. He extracted several large chips from the bag, using the same care he would have used in pulling the fuse on a bomb. They always tasted better when they were whole. As he crunched them, he stood at the table looking down at the letters.

Something was missing. He studied the letters, wishing that they were numbers, because if they were numbers he would know right away what was missing. But letters never seemed to add up to anything. How could you... "Ow!" he shouted as he miscued and bit his tongue instead of the potato chip. "Damn, that hurt!" He reached into his mouth with his index finger, touched the spot he had chomped down on, withdrew the finger, and looked at it. Well, at least there was no blood. But the worst was yet to come. Once you bit your tongue it swelled up, and it was certain you'd bite the same spot again.

He looked up quickly. How did you spell ow? O...W. He wrote it down and then he saw what was missing. Vowels.

There weren't any vowels. Now he sat down and wrote out the letters again, this time leaving space between each one.

c l d n d l n l y b v d g r n d

b r y d b n s n d d t r z r b f n d

Vaguely, he remembered one of his teachers having said that e was the most common letter. He wrote down the vowels; *a, e, i, o,* and *u.* The only way he could see to attack this was to try each vowel until he could make a word.

You didn't need much math to understand that it was going to take him close to forever, but for now it was all he could think of to try. You had to have a system to break a code. He wrote *cal, cel, cil, col, cul.* Then, before he tried a vowel between the next two letters, he tried to make a word by using the next consonant.

Cald, celd, cild, cold...cold. Was that it? But maybe he should have started with a vowel. Heck, plenty of words started with vowels. He tried the combinations but nothing made sense. He wrote down *Cold* as the first word, crossed off the first two letters, and this time started with a vowel. The word popped right out at him. *And. Cold and....* All right! Now he was getting somewhere. But was he really? Weren't there lots of other possible combinations? Never mind, he told himself. Just keep going and see where it leads. Then show the letters to Maria and see what she comes up with.

Next letters: *l n.* He began with a vowel.

Aln, eln, iln, oln, uln. Nothing there. He put the vowels between the letters.

Lan, Len, Lin, Lon, Lun. This looked a lot more likely than the first set, and suddenly he could see a number of possible words. Okay. What to add next? He looked back at the original letters. The next two were *l* and *y*. Lots of words ended in *ly*, so he tried that first.

*Lanly, lenly, linly, lonly, lun...*wait! *Lonely.* That was it! *Cold and lonely.* Yes!

Okay, what was next. He looked at the letters left and the last four in the first line drew his eye. *Grnd....* Huh, *grnd.* Okay, four consonants. What about putting a vowel in the middle? It seemed as good as any other place to start. *Grand, grind, grond, grend, grund.* It was getting a lot more complicated. He had two words, *grand* and *grind* and three that looked like they could be the ends of longer words. Suddenly he wished he'd paid a lot better attention in English. The *nd* on the end could be another and. But that would mean it ended a line and that didn't make any sense. Or did it? Time to look at the letters he'd skipped over.

Bvd. What the heck did that mean? Underwear? He laughed to himself. No, probably not underwear.

Abvd,ebvd, obvd, ibvd, ubvd. He tried pronouncing them but only the first combination sounded like a word. *Abovd...*he tried it again, saying it over and over and then suddenly he saw it. There were two words. *Above* and then the *d* could stand for *the. Cold and lonely above the...*he ran through the list of *g* words and nothing made any sense. Still, he had a line that made sense when he read it, and he had uncovered two terrific clues. *D* stood for the, and *nd* stood for and.

Back to *grnd.* He began by saying each sentence out loud, and when he got to *grnd* he stopped and said it again and then again "*Grund, Grund, Gr...Ground*! And there it was, or at least there was something that could be read and understood, even if he didn't know what it meant. He stood up and walked across the kitchen, staring blankly out the window at the field.

*Cold and lonely above the ground...*what did it mean? Did it mean anything at all, or had he even got it right? There were so many other possibilities. He shrugged. Nothing to do but get at it. Maybe the next line would make it come clear. He sat at the table and looked down at the paper.

B r y d̲ b n s n̲d̲d̲ t r z r b f̲n̲ d̲

He underlined the *d*'s and *nd*'s and then wrote the line out again, *b r y the bns and the t r z r b e f and*. The first two combinations made sense, but the last didn't make any sense at all because again he was sure the line couldn't end with *and*. He rewrote the line, *bry the bns and the trzrbfnd*. Then he tried a shortcut, pronouncing each word the way he did with the rebusses that came on the insides of Dad's Ballantine Ale caps, but nothing popped into his mind, and he went back to work, adding in vowels. Peter was concentrating so hard that he didn't hear his father come in.

"What are you working on?" Tom asked as he crossed to the sink and took down the can of Boraxo.

"Breaking code," Peter said.

"Really? Now that sounds like fun."

"It's cool, but it's really tough." He didn't look up for fear the words might somehow disappear.

Tom finished washing his hands, took a towel from the drying rack, and walked to the table, standing behind Peter as he looked down at the papers. "How're you doing?"

"Okay," Peter said. He looked around. "Hey, don't peek!" Peter covered the words with his hands.

Tom laughed and stepped away from the table. "Okay, but when do I get a turn?"

"As soon as I finish."

"I love stuff like that," Tom said. He walked back to the sink and spread the towel on the rack to dry. "Let me know when you're finished," he said. "I promised your mother I'd make a start on painting the living room, but I got so busy on the car I forgot." He couldn't help glancing toward the papers on the table.

"Hey! I said no peeking."

"Looks pretty tough," Tom said.

"It is," Peter said, "but I've got a system."

"What kind of system?"

"I'm not telling. You have to figure it out on your own."

"Fair enough. It's more fun that way."

"And then we can compare notes and see who found the best system."

"I gotta warn you," Tom said. "I'm pretty good at stuff like that."

Peter smiled at the good natured chiding. "I got a great system, here, Dad, you're gonna have to be really sharp to come up with a better way to work it out. I can guarantee it."

Tom grinned back. "A guy as smart as you, I wouldn't doubt it for a second."

"I'll call you," Peter said.

"Okay."

He looked back down at the letters, but now his concentration had been broken. He reached for the chips and lemonade. Then he repeated the second line as best he could, saying it over and over, and then finally he picked up the pencil and wrote the line out again.

Bry the bns and the trzrbfnd. How many words was he looking for? Two stood out clearly, but in the last set of letters he thought there were at least two, maybe three. He ran the vowels at the front of the first three letters, but none of them looked very promising. He tried the vowels after the *b*. *Bar*...he wrote and then wrote it again with the *y* because he couldn't think of a two letter word with a *y* in it. *Bary, Bery, Biry, Bory, Bury*. And there it was. *Bury. Bury the BNS. Bans? Ben? Bins? Bons? Buns? Buns! Bury the buns!*

It cracked him up and he had to resort to more lemonade and chips before he could get back to work. The only other word he saw was *bins*, but that didn't make any sense. Peter scratched his head and looked down at the letters again. If the *s* was really a plural, wouldn't he need a vowel before it? And more words ended in *e* than in the other vowels.

He tried it. *Bones*. Wow! *Bury the bones and the...T R Z R B F N D*. What if the last word in the line rhymed with ground? He ran several possibilities through his mind, starting with *nd* and then when he added the *f*, it came clear... *found. Bury the bones and the TRZRB found.* He went back to the rebus technique, figuring that if it had worked once it might work again. But this time it didn't pop out at him. No matter where he put the emphasis, nothing seemed to make sense. And then without the least warning, it did. *Treasure?* Yes, yes, yes...that was it! He wrote out both lines.

Cold and lonely above the ground
Bury the bones and the treasure be found.

He stood up and began pacing back and forth. It was perfectly clear. All they had to do was find Little Louie's bones and bury them. He sat down at the table, and then quickly stood up, gathered his papers, and stuffed them into the top drawer of the cabinet by the door. He closed his note pad, tucked it into the pocket of his shorts, and very quietly opened the screen door and stepped outside. It was time, time to find the bones, time to go find out what kind of a hole Little Louie had crawled into.

He'd have felt a whole lot better if Maria and Brian were with him, but sometimes you just couldn't wait. He walked past the pond, hardly noticing the hot sun on his back as he marched up into the field, past the pines, and cut a straight line to where the path led down to the bog.

Not until he stepped into the woods did he feel anything unusual. It was almost as if his feet had gone out of control. Twice he stopped, refusing to move forward until he was sure nothing was forcing him to choose which direction to go.

At the edge of the bog he turned and walked to the place where Maria had come back to the shore. He turned one way and then the other, hoping that somehow, something would tell him which way to go. He slapped distractedly at a mosquito, wishing he'd remembered to spray on some bug dope, because the bugs were really thick by the bog, and even if he didn't like the smell of the stuff, it beat being sucked dry.

Finally, he turned and followed the path off toward the dump. He had expected some help, and though he couldn't have guessed what might provide it, he sure had expected something. Now all he could do was walk along, trying to dope out just what Little Louie might have done after he came off the bog. He looked up at the sharply rising bank to his right and shook his head. It was so steep he would have had to use the trees to pull himself up to the top, and Little Louie couldn't have done that, not with one arm useless and needing the other to carry the money. He'd have picked an easier route, and the easiest route was along the path, at least until the bank dropped off a couple of hundred feet ahead. He stopped where the ground to the right of the path rose very slowly up into the woods. Somewhere in here, he thought, though just where he could not tell. What he had to assume was that Little Louie would have headed for something he saw in the woods; some place where he could hide. But where? All he could see were the trees. There were no rocks, no ledges, nothing that would offer any cover.

Then, with no warning, less than ten feet away the raven called and Peter recoiled, his body jerking as if he'd been shot. His heart pounded so hard he could hear it hammering in his ears as the raven cackled at him again and then flew, coasting from the barren branch of an old dead beech and lighting on the low, sweeping branch of a big white pine.

When he next called, the rattling and cackling changed, and now Peter was sure the raven was talking to him again. He took out his pad and pencil and wrote it down as best he could.

F R S H T D Y N D G N T M R R W

The raven waited for what seemed a long time before he began again.

B L D Z D N L Y P T H T F L L W.

Then he paused for a moment and repeated the first line. Peter wrote it down again, deciding that it would give him some way to check himself.

Finally the bird called one last long, drawn out raven sort of rattle, dropped from the limb, and disappeared into the trees as a sudden cool gust of wind blew through the woods. Peter turned and looked behind him at the rapidly darkening sky. In the distance he could hear the faint growl of approaching thunder. With each growl the thunder seemed to come closer. It was a line squall, one of those fast-moving storms that swept past very quickly, but usually carried high winds and a lot of lightning. Peter decided that the shortest way home was the best way, and he bolted up the shallow rise, thinking more about the thunder than his footing, caught his toe on a root and went down with a thump, twisting his ankle and landing hard on his knees. As he pulled himself up, something caught his eye. Blood! His hands were covered with blood! But he couldn't find a cut anywhere. Then, looking past his hands he spotted the pool of blood on the ground. It was the same bright red color as the blood they had seen in the car.

That and the sound of thunder claps coming closer and closer, got him onto his feet and sore ankle or not, he ran — the branches slapping at his arms and legs and face as he raced for the field.

Once in the open he ran faster, spooked as thoroughly as a runaway horse, spooked both by the blood and his fear of getting caught in the open in a lightning storm. And now, behind him, he could hear the rain roaring across the woods like an onrushing train as he tried to beat it to the house.

He'd only just passed the pines when it overtook him and soaked him through in seconds. The cold rain washed away the sweat and ran down his face, cooling him, reviving him, giving him the strength to run faster, and just now he needed that badly because now he could see the flashes of lightning, and the thunderclaps were only seconds behind each flash.

Down the hill he came, barreling past the pond and turning at the barn for the house, just as the flash and the thunder came right together and he whirled to see an old pine out past the barn disintegrate in a flash of light, pieces of wood flying in all directions as the tree seemed to explode.

"Peter! Run, Peter! Run!" Sarah called from the house, but he needed no encouragement. He'd have set the world record for the twenty-five yard dash, if there were such an event, and he came tearing across the lawn, hurdling over a flower garden and then up onto the stone slab, and finally through the door and into the house.

"Are you all right?" Sarah asked.

"Sure. I'm fine. Nothing to worry about, Mom. Man, did you see that pine tree?" She had closed the door and he went to the window and pointed to the tree. "Look. The lightning blew it to smithereens!"

"Where the hell did that hit?" Tom asked as he walked into the kitchen and crossed to the windows.

"That old pine," Peter said as he pointed out the window.

"Whoa, that was some big bolt to do that much damage," Tom said. "It blew the whole top off!" He shook his head. "That is...awesome! That is definitely, totally awesome, as some folks around here would say."

Peter smiled around at his father. "Definitely, amazingly, totally, completely awesome!"

Even as they watched, the rain began to taper off, and then it stopped, and the sun came out strong and harsh, blasting through the black sky.

"Hey, look, a rainbow." Peter pointed out toward the end of the field and immediately a shiver ran up his spine. It ended in the grove of trees just above the bog.

"I haven't seen a line squall like that in years," Tom said.

Peter stood dead still, watching the rainbow, bright and full, arcing down into the woods beyond the field. And then slowly it began to fade and finally, when the rain stopped, it disappeared altogether. Talk about freaky.

"Peter," Sarah said. "You are soaked through."

He looked down. "That was some wicked rain," he said. "For a minute, when I was out by the pines, I could hardly see the house. And then that lightning bolt came down and I thought the sky was falling. Wow! I can't believe what it did to that pine."

"Well, go get changed," Sarah said, and as Peter turned toward the front of the house, she added, "and don't leave your wet clothes in a pile on your floor. Bring them back down so I can run them through with the next wash."

"Okay," he said as he fished the note pad from his pocket. It was lucky he had taken a pencil instead of a pen, he thought, because the rain would have made the ink run, but it hadn't affected the lead at all and he could read the letters clearly.

Upstairs he changed his clothes and then, forgetting what his mother had said about leaving them in a pile on the floor, he sat down at his desk and began trying to dope out the letters. This time the task did not seem so daunting. After all, he'd figured out the first two lines pretty quickly, so how hard could this be?

Not until he picked up the pencil did he notice that the blood on his hands was gone. Had it been the rain? No. It was just like before. As soon as you left the woods the blood disappeared.

He wrote the letters on a sheet of paper.

F R S H T D N D Y G N T M R R W.
B L D Z D N L Y P T H T F L L W.

Using the same system he began to pull words from the jumbled letters. *F r s h t d y and g n t m r r w.* The first word was easy. *Fresh.* The next word came just as fast. *Today.* He concentrated on the last seven letters, repeating them over and over. At first nothing came to him and then slowly, as he said them out loud, they began to make some sort of sense. And then, almost magically, they simply fell into place.

Fresh today gone tomorrow

The second line came very quickly. *Bld is the nly pth t fllw.* He tried pronouncing the words and the first ones popped into his head: *Blood is the....only* . He added a vowel to *pth*. *Path*. The rest he simply wrote down as if the words had been written out for him.

Blood is the only path to follow.

Fresh today gone tomorrow.
Blood is the only path to follow

He stared at the lines for a minute or so, deciding that something wasn't quite right, and then he reversed them.

Blood is the only path to follow
Fresh today gone tomorrow

Tomorrow? Was that the day Little Louie had died? Would it really be gone? They couldn't take the chance, they had to go look today. But now, he really did not want to go alone, and there was no telling when Maria and Brian would get back. If they got home in time for supper, they could at least go look till it got dark, and that would give them nearly two hours. For now all he could do was wait...and that was about the last thing he wanted to do.

"Peter!" Sarah called up the stairs. "Don't forget those wet clothes."

"Okay, Mom," he called back. He picked up the clothes and carried them downstairs to the laundry room. From there he wandered back out to the kitchen. He felt as jumpy as he did when he was sneaking a can of soda. What he needed was something to do and then as he looked out he spotted the basketball hoop on the barn. All right! Shoot some hoops! He ran out to the barn, got the ball and went to work, practicing his moves with the ball, practicing shooting off the dribble, trying to control his position in the air so he always came up square to the basket.

It worked. By focusing, by narrowing his concentration, he shut everything else out until there was nothing but the ball and the hoop.

Chapter Fourteen

From the Land of the Dead

Only because Sarah had planned an early supper by the pond, were Maria and Brian home by four-thirty. It took less than half-an-hour to eat, and then they raced upstairs to stand by Peter's desk looking down at the letters.

"What do they mean?" Maria asked.

"It's a code," Peter said. He dropped down onto his bed and tucked his hands behind his head, smiling with obvious self-satisfaction. "You have to work it out."

"Did you work it out?" Brian asked.

"Yeah, but I wanted you guys to try it and see what you came up with."

"Where did you get it?"

"From the raven."

"But you promised you wouldn't go!"

"I had to, Maria. I just had the feeling that I'd learn something, and I think I did."

"What?"

"I'm not sure. It's in the code. I worked it out, but I could be wrong, and that's why you guys have to work it out."

Maria shook her head. "I'm no good at stuff like that," she said. "All I see is a bunch of garbled letters that don't make any sense." She looked around at Peter. "Do we have to do this now?"

He nodded. "Right now, if I'm right."

She shook her head. "I don't even know where to start."

"It's not a big deal, Maria. First you set up a system and then keep plugging letters in until you can make them into words. Even Dad's gonna do it, but I don't know whether he'll get it done today or not, and it has to be done right now." He sat up. "There's another way to look at it. When I worked out the first two lines I used a system, but the second time I didn't have to. I just sounded out the words the way we do with those bottle caps from Dad's beer."

"Two times? You went out there alone twice?"

He shrugged. "It was okay," he said.

Maria looked at her younger brother as if she'd never seen him before. "That was pretty brave, Peter."

He shrugged. "I just couldn't wait."

Brian glanced down dubiously at the letters on the pad, shook his head, then walked away, and sat in the chair by the window. It was almost as bad as crossword puzzles and he hated it when his teacher had them make up their own. It seemed like a big waste of time, and usually he got pissed off and had to be forced to finish.

Maria pulled up a chair and sat at the desk. She rested her head on her hands as she stared at the letters. At first they made no sense, and then slowly, as if they were appearing out of a deep mist, she could see the words, and she picked up the pencil and began writing.

Cold and lonely above the ground
Bury the bones and the treasure be found.

That's incredible," Peter said as he shook his head. It took me almost an hour to get that. How could you do that? Damn, Maria, that really makes me mad. I work out this awesome system, and you just write it out."

"Did you get the same thing?" Maria asked.

"Exactly the same. Word-for-word...how did you do that?"

Maria shook her head. "I'm not sure. Suddenly I could just see the words. I think you were right about looking at it like a rebus."

"Try the next one," Brian said. His respect for his older sister had just risen substantially. It climbed even higher when a few seconds later she wrote out the second message.

Peter stood up and looked over her shoulder at the paper on the desk. "Man, how do you do that? I don't understand. I had to work my butt off to figure that out, and then you just sit down and it's done." He grinned. "But then you always get those rebuses before I do."

"Is it the same?" she asked.

"You could break enemy codes for the Army," Peter said. "I can't believe you did that so easily." He unfolded his paper and set it next to Maria's. "See? They're the same." He scratched his head. "How do you do that?"

"I just let my mind go blank. I do the same thing on a test

when I have multiple choice questions." She studied the two papers. "If this means what I think it means, we haven't got a whole lot of time. Am I right about that, Peter?"

"What do you think it means?" Brian asked.

"That we have until dark tonight to find Little Louie's bones," she said.

"That's what I think too," Peter said.

"How much time is there till dark?" Maria asked.

"Maybe two hours. If it stays clear, maybe a little longer," Peter said.

Maria looked out the window across the field toward the bog, then shivered. "I wish I could forget about all of this. I wish it had never happened."

"Me too," Peter said, "but we have to find out."

Maria nodded. "Let's go, but instead of going out through the kitchen, let's use the back door in the living room."

They trooped down the stairs, turned toward the door that opened to the north, and stopped. Because the room was being painted, the door was blocked with what looked like a ton of furniture.

"Now what do we do?" Peter shoved his hands deep into his pockets. "One look at us and they'll know something is up. Especially Mom. She's got eyes like a laser."

"I think we should tell Dad," Brian said.

"He won't believe us, Bri," Peter said, "and we'll just lose a lot of time trying to explain it. If we're gonna do this, we've got to do it on our own. We're the only ones who can see the blood, and that means we're the only ones who can follow the trail."

"I'm kinda scared," Brian said.

"We all are," Maria said.

Tom walked into the living room. "I was looking for you

guys. That was one tough word puzzle. It took me quite awhile, but I think I figured it out. " He looked down at the piece of paper in his hand, flipped down his glasses and read it out loud. "Is that it? Did I figure it out?"

"You got it, Dad," Peter said. "Perfect."

"What does it mean?"

It was a question he had not expected, and Peter thought quickly. "It's from a book I'm reading. I won't know until I read some more."

Tom smiled. "Sounds like an exciting book."

"It is." Peter turned toward the kitchen.

"Where are you guys going?"

"I gotta show Maria and Brian the place I found to build a tree fort before it gets too dark."

"If you need a hand with that fort let me know," Tom said. "I built a couple of beauties when I was a kid."

"We will," Maria said, and then they turned and left the house.

Peter crossed the driveway to the tool shed on the side of the barn where he picked out a short handled shovel and a burlap sack. Using the barn to screen them from the house they headed up the old tote road into the woods. Even with the sun still over an hour from setting it was nearly dark in the church-like quiet of the spruce. They did not speak, but walked quickly along, pushing aside the heavy green branches which slashed out over the road here and there, holding them for each other, and then regrouping. No one wanted to be last and yet no one wanted to be first either. Not until they reached the open hardwoods did they talk.

"Peter, that was really fast thinking," Maria said. "I couldn't think of anything to say."

"I don't know." Brian said. "Dad's pretty smart."

"So what's he gonna do, Bri, follow us?" Peter said. He rested the handle of the shovel over his shoulder.

"He could," Brian said, and from the almost hopeful way he said it they knew he was more spooked than they had thought.

"It'll be okay, Bri," Peter said.

"Peter's right, Bri, "Maria said, trying to keep her voice calm and steady. But the truth was, she'd have felt much better if Dad had gone with them. The closer they got, the more certain she grew that something truly terrible was waiting for them. And yet, even as she thought that, she told herself that it was all in her imagination. Visions and spirits and ghosts and monsters were the stuff of books and stories told at night around campfires, nothing more. As soon as you got up and walked around, you weren't afraid anymore. The same thing happened in a scary movie. As soon as it was over you stopped being scared...until you climbed into bed and turned out the lights, and the images from the movie began to jump into your mind.

They came out where the car had sat, crossed the field, and took the path down to the bog.

"Now, follow me," Peter said. He turned and walked along the trail by the edge of the bog, stopping where he had found the blood. "Look carefully for any sign of blood. That'll tell us which way to go."

Maria scanned slowly through the trees "I don't see the raven anywhere," Maria said.

The soft distant sound of her voice stopped Peter cold. He looked at her carefully, studying her face for any sign of the trance which had closed over her before. "How do you feel?" Peter asked.

"Weird. Almost like I'm floating." She put her hand to

her forehead, then reached out with her other hand and leaned against a tree. "I feel kind of dizzy, but not really dizzy. It's like the pressure I get sometimes just before I'm going to get a headache."

"That means the spirit is trying to get into your brain," Brian said. "I read in a book that it can't get in unless you let it in. You have to keep your mind working. Keep thinking about things, don't let your mind go blank."

"Concentrate on looking for the blood," Peter said.

But it was growing very strong and her head had begun to ache. "He's coming," she said. "He's taking me over again and I can't stop him."

"You can, Maria! You have to!" Peter said.

"But it's so much easier not to fight him. He's so terribly strong...so terribly strong...." She grabbed Peter's right arm with both hands, her grip as strong as a pair of vise-grip pliers. "Peter! Peter help me. Help me fight him off. Do something, anything, he's so close, so close..."

Peter grabbed her by the shoulders and shook her, hollering at her, calling her name, but he could see her slipping steadily away.

"Maria likes Eddie Porter!" Brian shouted. "Maria thinks he's the hottest of the hot, the cutest of the cute..."

"I'm gonna kill you!" She shouted, whirling away from Peter. "I'm gonna mash you up like squash and feed you to the...the...the turtles!"

Just as she grabbed him, the raven dropped down from the tree above them, lighting on a branch almost directly at eye level. He sat perfectly still, head cocked to the side, his cold, beady black eyes watching them.

"Maria, are you okay?" Brian asked.

"No, I'm not okay, I am totally, totally, totally pissed off.

I..." she looked around at Peter, back at Brian and laughed. "It's gone...I'm okay."

"Wow...." Peter shook his head, stuffed his hands into his pockets, and squeezed his elbows against his sides. "Bri that was incredible. Man, talk about dealing with pressure. I had no idea what to do."

"What did he do?" Maria looked mystified.

"He got you pissed off," Peter said, "and when he got you pissed off, you focused so hard on him that the spirit couldn't get in." He pointed to the raven. "See, there's the bird and the way it works, when the bird's here, Little Louie's spirit is caught in the bird."

Maria shook her head. "Good old Bri comes through in the pinch. How did you think of that?"

"I just tried the first thing that came into my head. It's just a good thing that I've had so much practice pissing you off." he grinned. "Boy, Maria, you went off like a sky rocket. It was awesome!"

They laughed and the laughter helped considerably to relieve the pressure, but it did not last long.

"Look!" Maria said as she pointed to the trail just ahead. The blood shone brightly from the green leaves of a maple sapling.

They ran to that spot, and then quickly picked up another spot and then another, the blood glistening in the summer evening sunlight that filtered down through the trees. Where the high bank to their right tapered down sharply into only a shallow rise, the trail turned to the right and wandered off into the woods.

As they moved slowly through the trees, Maria kept track of the raven, following them now, quiet but for the rush of air that slipped past its feathers as it flew from tree to tree. And now she was aware of a new uneasiness, and this time she had the feeling that they had either overlooked something, or not understood something, or both. Did they have any idea how much danger they were facing? Had they really stopped to consider that this spirit belonged to a cold-blooded killer, a man as evil and cruel as any who had ever lived? She shivered, the emptiness in her stomach making her certain now that something dreadful lay just ahead. God, this was stupid, really, really stupid. They should never have come out here alone. They should've brought Dad with them. And yet, had there been another choice? Whenever he was around, the weird stuff all disappeared. Clearly, it was up to them to find out where this would lead.

Peter stopped, turning his head this way and that as he scanned the woods ahead. The trunks of the big oaks and pines seemed like the legs of giants, but that was only because of their size. In truth the woods did not frighten him in the least. It was not, after all, some Snow-White woods, some cartoonist's idea of a forest.

"What are we looking for?" Brian asked.

"I'm not sure," Peter said. "Remember when Maria asked Dad about what the woods might have looked like then, and he told us about the damage the hurricane had done? Maybe Little Louie found a place to hide in the roots of those trees. What I'm trying to figure out is what those trees would look like today."

"Brian?" Maria turned toward him. "You're the nature expert. What would they look like?"

"The roots would rot and fall to the ground first and then each year everything would be covered by another layer of leaves. A book I read on forestry said you're not supposed to leave slash piles because they're a good place for fires to start. It takes years for a slash pile to rot down, but it takes even longer for a tree to rot away. I guess I'd look for some kind of big lump buried in the leaves."

"Like that?" Maria pointed to a lump that rose several feet above the forest floor. And then, as they looked around, they saw several lumps together and they all had the same shape; sloping off sharply to the east and tapering to the west.

"Yeah," Brian said."Exactly like that."

"Why do they all point the same way?" Maria asked. "What could cause that?"

"Wind throw," Brian said. "Hurricane winds come from the northeast so the trees would have fallen to the southwest. That means the bottoms of their roots would have to face northeast."

"Which means that the bottom of the tree would have to face that way," Peter said. "Is that right, Bri?"

"It would have to," Brian said. He looked around. "There sure are a lot of them." He pointed to clumps here and there, at the same time puzzling over why two other enormous trees had not gone down, and whether that was somehow part of this. But as he thought about it, he was sure it wasn't. Stuff like that happened all the time in storms, especially in twisters, and a hurricane was nothing but a giant twister.

"Look for blood," Peter said. "I'll look straight ahead, and Maria, you look left and Brian, you look right."

They moved one step at a time, working their eyes in and out. Peter found the first spot just ahead, and then several steps later Maria found one off to the left. They went that way and suddenly the direction was clear. Twenty or so feet ahead they could see a clump of mounds which interlocked into one large mound at the end.

"There," Peter said. "That's it. That's the place."

They ran to the spot and Peter swung the shovel into position and drove the blade into the soil.

"Peter, stop. Wait a second," Maria said.

"Why? It's getting late."

"Just wait a second!"

He left the shovel sticking into the ground, and as he always did when he was frustrated, drove his hands deep into his pockets.

"I think there's something else. I can feel something in the air. It's cold and damp. It's like something from beneath the ground is trying to get hold of me and drag me down. I can feel it around my ankles, like somebody's icy cold hands..." Suddenly she looked upward, staring at the Raven, its eyes so bright they seemed to glow in the dim woods.

Brian's face had grown pale, and it wasn't going to take much to send him running for home.

"Jeez, Maria," Peter said, "will you cut it out? You're scaring poor old Bri half-to-death." He looked around. "I don't see anything, I don't even hear anything." But he did not go on digging, instead backing away a step from the shovel, and looking around in every direction, and holding his breath so he could hear the slightest sound. In his right pocket, his fingers curled around the bullet he had found earlier. He must have transferred it from his wet shorts after the rain, but he could not remember having done that. The bullet felt oddly warm in his hand. "Com'on, Maria, we haven't got much time. It's gonna start to get dark."

Suddenly she thought about the rhymes from the raven. "Peter! Whatever you do, don't dig." She looked around for the raven, but she could not see him. "The rhymes," she said. "I think they mean more than we thought, I mean, I think that they have more than one meaning."

"What?" Peter stood slouched, showing his irritation with Maria over what he regarded as foolishness. The words meant what they said and that was all there was to it.

"Listen," she said. "Cold and lonely above the ground, bury the bones and the treasure be found. He doesn't say *his* bones. He just says bones. They could be our bones! Maybe this is a trap. Maybe he's just been waiting for someone else to kill."

"I don't know," Peter said and though he tried not to show it, the idea had plainly worried him. "I think we oughta start digging and see what happens, before it gets too dark."

"Fresh today and gone tomorrow, blood is the path to follow. His blood or our blood?"

"I'm getting kinda nervous," Brian said.

A sudden sharp hiss stopped them and they stood looking around, trying to figure out where it had come from, and suddenly they saw a strange iridescent fog rising from the ground around the blade of the shovel. It came faster and faster, the hiss growing louder, and then in the air above the mound, they could see a figure start to form.

"Oh my God, it's him...." Maria put her hand to her mouth.

"Welcome," the vision said. "Glad youse could make it. I been a long time here without no company, but now I'm gonna have company forever." And then he laughed in a raspy, guttural voice that made them shiver. "Don't try to run, on account of you can't. I've took care of that. I got power. I got power nobody ever dreamed of. The fact of it is, if Id'a had power like this here when I was alive, I never woulda got dead."

"Run!" Peter shouted and he turned to run, but his feet wouldn't come free. He turned toward the house, opening his mouth to scream for help, but he could not raise his voice above a whisper. How could they have been so dumb? How could they have thought they could just come walking in and dig up the money?

The spirit seemed to sway back and forth, now dim and blurry, and now bright and sharply focused. "Let's see. Which one of youse am I gonna pick first."

A long tendril of mist began to glide toward them, slowly darkening, and then they could see it was an arm.

"It won't hurt long," he said. "Only when I first touch you, and then all I have to do is pull you out of this world and into the land of the dead."

"You're dead. You were killed. Why don't you stay dead?" Brian said.

The image focused on Brian. "Hey, smart kid there. It's a good question. I think it's on account of the bullet didn't kill me. I lost a lot of blood and it made me weak and I died real, real slow."

"But why kill us?" Peter asked.

"Cause that's what I do...kill people...I done it since I was ten and I stuck another kid with a knife at a birthday party. Best one I ever went to."

Suddenly he grew very bright. "The girl. I'll take the girl first!" Both arms reached slowly out for Maria and she tried to scream, but now she could make no sound at all.

Peter's fingers wrapped around the warm bullet and he pulled it from his pocket and held it up. "Is this the bullet that didn't kill you?"

The spirit wavered and pulled back.

Peter, bolder now as the spirit began to shrink back, moved his right foot, and suddenly he could walk, and he took a step forward. "I asked you a question," Peter said.

"Where did you find that?"

"On the ground by your car."

"Get it away from me."

Peter held it closer, stretching his arm as far out as he could reach. "What are you afraid of? Are you afraid of this bullet. Are you afraid that after all this time it's come back to finish the job?"

"You can't stop me! That bullet won't stop me this time anymore than it did the first time!" The base of the spirit glowed an eerie red where it disappeared into the ground. Then suddenly, quickly, the color spread upward and the spirit suddenly doubled in size.

Maria and Brian shrunk away from the fierce yellow eyes as Peter waved the bullet in the air. "You won't escape it this time, Louie. This time the bullet will get you!"

The voice was suddenly deep and very loud. "That bullet ain't got no power over me! It went right through me once and it'll go right through me again!"

Peter smiled and drew back his arm. "But this bullet has your blood on it. It knows where to find you."

"No, don't!" the spirit cried.

Using every bit of strength he had, Peter threw the bullet directly at the heart of Little Louie LaMontaigne. All the time spent playing baseball paid off. His aim was perfectly true, and when the bullet hit, a great bright light exploded in the middle of the image, followed by a long, drawn out wail, and the colors began to swirl, the bright reds and yellows fading into blues and greens and then into gray, and then it began to swirl like a tornado, spinning faster and faster as it rose above the ground, climbing higher and higher, above the treetops, into the sky.

They stood in the sudden hush, unwilling to move, even to speak, until they were sure it was gone.

"You did it!" Maria said. "You destroyed it, Peter. You absolutely obliterated it!"

"What did you throw?" Brian asked, still not sure what had happened.

Peter shook his head and looked down at his right hand. "The bullet. It was the same bullet that wounded Little Louie. I found it this afternoon over where the car used to be." He looked up, first at Brian and then at Maria. "Are you both okay?" he asked.

"I think so," Maria said.

"I'm fine," Brian said. "Perfectly fine. No problemo." He rubbed his eyes and looked over at the shovel. "Did I really see what I thought I did, I mean a ghost coming out of the ground by the shovel?"

Maria nodded.

He stuffed his hands deep into his pockets. "I always thought I wanted to see a ghost," he said, "and now I think I wish I hadn't."

"Why?" Maria asked.

"Because now I have to believe in ghosts, and that makes things a lot more complicated."

Peter shook his head and looked down at his hand. "Look," he said. "It left a mark." On the inside of his thumb and first two fingers the silhouette of the bullet stood out plainly, a dark purple color, more like a birthmark than a bruise. "I wonder if it will ever go away," he said. "I sure hope so...."

"How did you know the bullet would work?" Maria asked.

He shrugged. "It was all I had, and then he was scared of it. And suddenly I could move my feet, but I couldn't get close enough. All I could think to do was throw it at him. It still had his blood on it."

"It was like some kind of awful, terrible nightmare," Brian

said. "Only a whole lot worse."

Maria reached out and pinched him.

"Ow, hey, what the heck, Maria...."

"You felt it, right?"

"Of course I felt it!"

"Then it means you're not dreaming." She looked at the shovel still sticking up from the ground. "I'm sorry, Bri," she said.

"It's okay," he said, "but there must be an easier way than that to find out if I'm awake. I hate getting pinched almost as much as I hate getting a Dutch rub."

Peter and Maria laughed.

"It isn't funny, either. I think you're both a couple of perverts."

Peter wrapped his hands around the handle of the shovel. "Time to dig," he said and it broke the spell, though even as they concentrated on digging, they stopped now and then to look around and to listen. But the woods had assumed the shape of a summer evening, quiet except for the distant tapering call of a veery and the wonderfully plaintive call of a lone hermit thrush.

And the digging was surprisingly easy, because the soil was hardly soil at all, but instead, the composted remains of fifty-seven years of fallen leaves. As they dug, they opened a tunnel that twisted between the old root clumps of the trees, and then suddenly the shovel struck something hard and instead of digging straight in, Peter started sweeping the blade sideways, slowly exposing the last remains of Little Louie LaMontaigne.

"Wow, look at that," Peter said. "A perfect human skeleton."

Brian pointed to the right shoulder. "That's where the

bullet hit him. See how the bones are all smashed up."

"Cool," Peter said. "Really cool. I wish I had one of these hanging in my room. Cool! Get a black light and...."

"Ugh! That is gross, Peter, really, really gross!"

"Hey," Brian said, "Where's the money?"

Peter bent down and looked carefully. "I don't know. It's gotta be here...no, wait! *Bury the bones and the treasure be found.* "We have to bury the bones."

"You're not gonna touch them, are you?" Maria shrank back. "How could you do that?" She stepped back away from the skeleton, wanting nothing to do with bones of any kind, least of all the bones of Little Louie LaMontaigne.

"Maybe we shouldn't," Peter said.

Brian looked off to the west at the sun, just settling into the tree tops. "It's gonna get dark."

"We can come back in the morning," Peter said.

"No." Brian folded his arms over his chest. "It's got to be done now. By morning it'll be all different again." He turned and started for the skeleton just as a ray of sunlight shot down through the trees and illuminated the bones.

"Look!" Maria pointed to a smooth patch of black leather just beyond the skull. "What's that?"

Peter stepped quickly past Brian, and taking care not to touch Little Louie's bones, brushed away the soil and the leaves. Carefully, he picked up the old leather satchel and carried it back into the open.

"Is the money in it, do you think?" Brian asked.

"It must be," Peter said.

"It's got to be," Maria said.

"What are you waiting for?" Brian asked.

"I don't know, I just feel a little strange..."

"Jeez, Peter, it's no big deal," Brian said.

But Peter was not convinced, and he stepped back scanning the treetops and the sky. "I just think it isn't over yet, I think there's something more waiting for us, something even scarier."

"I can feel it too," Maria said. "Suppose the spirit isn't gone. Suppose it was only a trick."

"I'm not waiting," Brian said, "because if we wait much longer we're gonna be out here in the dark, and I don't like being in the woods in the dark." He looked around, scanning the trees. "Especially this night." He squatted by the bag and tried to open the catch, but it was frozen shut, and try as he might, Brian couldn't pry it apart.

"Don't, please don't," Maria said.

"Give me your Swiss Army knife, Peter."

"Maybe Maria's right, Bri."

Without another word, Brian reached around, grabbed the shovel, and used the blade to pop open the latch. As the bag flew open they heard the raven screech and then scream, and they all dropped to the ground as it dove down at them, wheeled and came back for another pass, gaining speed each time, slashing at them with its great, sharp beak. Then it wheeled for another pass. Without taking his eyes off the bird, Peter groped for something to use as a weapon. His hand closed on something hard and when the bird, coming swift as an arrow, got within range, he rolled to his feet and swung his weapon just as he would a baseball bat, stepping into it, his wrists rolling, his hips popping open, his eyes focused on the raven as he delivered the blow.

The collision was spectacular, producing a great shower of sparks and a sharp crack and a brilliant blue-white flash of light. The sudden burst of energy blew Peter ten feet backward, knocking him to the ground.

For an instant the raven seemed to just float in the air and then slowly it twisted toward the ground, whirling faster and faster until all they could see was a dark blur. When it touched the leaves it exploded upward and vanished in the rapidly darkening air.

Only then did Peter look down at the weapon in his hand...Little Louie LaMontaigne's left thigh bone!

"Wow!" Brian said. "You used one of the bones!"

Quick as a striking snake, Peter scrambled to his feet and threw the bone back toward the skeleton.

"Look, look at that!" Maria pointed at Little Louie's bones. "They're falling apart."

As they watched, the bones simply turned to a dry, gray dust, and then the dust began to work its way down into the soil. In seconds there was nothing left of Little Louie LaMontaigne. All that remained was the bag.

Peter stepped past the bones, picked up the satchel with both hands, and carried it to where he had dropped the sack. Then he opened the top and gasped.

"What is it?" Maria asked, steeping back quickly.

"Money," he grinned. "A whole lot of money!" He opened the satchel as wide as it would go as Brian and Maria leaned in closer. It was full almost to the top with carefully wrapped packages of thousand dollar bills.

"Awesome...." Peter said. "It was true. The money was here all along, right where the rainbow ended."

"Rainbow?" Maria looked around at him.

"After the squall when the lightning struck the big white pine on the other side of the pond, there was a rainbow, and it ended right here."

"I think I'm glad you didn't tell me that," Maria said.

Brian picked up a package, turning it over and looking at

at it carefully. "This stuff is worth even more than it says on the bills. These are silver certificates, not Federal Reserve Notes."

"What's the difference?" Peter asked.

"You used to be able to turn them in for silver...pure silver. You remember the silver dollars grandpa gave us? I read up on money to find out more about them. Collectors are always looking for silver certificates, and they'll pay extra for them, even though the government won't give them silver anymore. It's a really big deal."

"Does Dad know about stuff like that?" Maria asked.

"Sure," Brian said. "We've got a book in our library all about it."

"Give me a hand, Maria," Peter said as he picked up the bag from the bottom. "Hold the sack open."

She held it for him as he carefully slid the satchel into the burlap sack. Then he threw it over his shoulder and turned for the house.

"Wait," Maria said. She picked up the shovel. "This ought to be covered." She scooped the soft black soil back over the dust of Little Louie LaMontaigne, thoroughly covering the area between the old stumps. Finally she sprinkled leaves over the soil.

"It looks like a graveyard for monsters," Brian said.

Maria nodded. "It is."

They turned away then, walking off through the woods, cutting a direct line toward the house. It looked especially warm and friendly as it sat bathed by the last rays of the setting sun.

"Wait till Mom and Dad see this," Maria said.

Peter laughed. "It's gonna blow their doors off."

"It's also," Brian said, "gonna make it a lot harder to tell us we can't have two dogs."

They laughed together as they walked across the field, each of them coming up with things they would buy with the money, even though they were certain they'd not be given free rein.

"Hey!" Tom called, as they walked into the yard. "You're not gonna believe this, but all of a sudden the car just started right up. Listen to that! It runs like a top." He was so excited he hadn't noticed the shovel and the burlap sack. "I wish I knew what I did. I mean I just decided that I'd give it a try, and I came out and stepped on the starter and it ran. It never hesitated. It just turned over like a brand new engine! Incredible!"

"Do you think..." Peter said.

"Of course," Maria said.

Just then Tom noticed the sack. "Now what are you guys lugging home. What did you do? Make another bottle run?"

"Dad," Maria said. "We've got a little surprise here...."

About the Author

Robert Holland has a B.A. in history from the University of Connecticut and an M.A. in English from Trinity College. He studied writing under Rex Warner at UConn and under Stephen Minot at Trinity.

He has worked as a journalist, a professor, a stock broker, an editor, and from time to time, anything he could make a buck at. He hunts, he is a fly fisherman, a wood-carver, a cabinet maker, and he plays both classical and folk guitar.

While he was never a great athlete, he played with enthusiasm and to some extent overcame his lack of natural ability by teaching himself how to play and then practicing.

Sometime during college he decided he wanted to be a writer and has worked at it ever since, diverting the energy he once poured into sports to becoming not only a writer, but a writer who understands the importance of craft. Like all writers he reads constantly, not only because, as Ernest Hemingway once said, "you have to know who to beat," but because it is the only way to gather the information which every writer must have in his head, and because it is a way to learn how other writers have developed the narrative techniques which make stories readable, entertaining, and meaningful.

He lives in Woodstock, Connecticut with his wife, Leslie, his daughter Morgan, his son Gardiner, four Labrador retrievers, four cats, two guinea pigs, and six chickens.